I'll Never Be
Long Gone

ALSO BY THOMAS CHRISTOPHER GREENE

Mirror Lake

I'll Never Be Long Gone

Thomas Christopher Greene

WILLIAM MORROW
An Imprint of HarperCollins*Publishers*

HarperCollins books may be purchased for educational, business, or sales promotional use. For information please write: Special Markets Department, HarperCollins Publishers, 10 East 53rd Street, New York, NY 10022.

FIRST EDITION

Designed by Sarah Gubkin

Printed on acid-free paper

Library of Congress Cataloging-in-Publication Data

Greene, Thomas Christopher, 1968–
    I'll never be long gone : a novel / Thomas Christopher Greene.—1st ed.
      p. cm.
    ISBN-13: 978-0-6-076580-4
    ISBN-10: 0-06-076580-1
    1. Suicide victims—Family relationships—Fiction. 2. Fathers and sons—Fiction. 3. Fathers—Death—Fiction. 4. Brothers—Fiction. I. Title

PS3607.R453I44 2005
813'.6—dc22

2005047178

05 06 07 08 09 WBC/RRD 10 9 8 7 6 5 4 3 2 1

— For Tia —

Bury me in the trunk of your car.
I won't be ready to sleep.
I'll drive underground,
follow your footsteps around town,
until I track you down.
Vanishing and reappearing,
I'll never be long gone.
Bury me wherever you are.
I don't want to have to search that far.
I know a place where we could go,
where it always snows,
but it's never cold there.
Vanishing and reappearing,
I'll never be long gone.

The Butterflies of Love, "I'll Never Be Long Gone"

A Note on Place

As in my novel *Mirror Lake*, the Eden, Vermont, of *I'll Never Be Long Gone* is not meant to represent the actual geography of that very real Northeast Kingdom town. Rather, my Eden is a composite of places I love, places I know well, and places I have created out of whole cloth.

Thomas Christopher Greene
Montpelier, Vermont
January 22, 2005

I'll Never Be
Long Gone

Book One

PROLOGUE

That night while they slept, the heavy clouds from the west crossed the mountains and into Eden, and with them came the rain, a cold, driving rain that fell in sheets and rattled the twelve-pane windows in the bedroom the two brothers shared in the old farmhouse. Charlie slept fitfully. At one point the rain was falling so hard it woke him, and he rose up on his elbows and watched it streaming down the windows and the light outside was gray and subdued with dawn. He was able to fall back asleep but he tossed and turned and sometime that morning he woke suddenly, sensing his mother before he even heard her, before she opened the door to their room, and then she was there and he knew from the look on her face that something was wrong, that something was terribly wrong.

"Mom," he said, "what is it?"

"It's your father, Charlie. He went into the woods."

Charlie sat up, rubbed his eyes; ran a hand through his hair. "So?"

"He had a gun."

"I don't get it."

"Hunting season is two months away, Charlie. I'm worried he might—"

Charlie stood quickly and he felt light-headed. "I'll get him," he said, and by now their voices had woken Owen and he was looking at them with the slight daze of sleep.

"What's up?" Owen said.

"Get dressed," said Charlie.

"What's going on?"

"Just get dressed. Hurry."

Charlotte left the room and Charlie heard her footsteps going down the stairs. He slipped on a pair of jeans and a T-shirt, and outside he could see that it was still raining, though not with the fury it had during the night. Owen climbed out of bed and followed Charlie's lead, sliding into his jeans, pulling a shirt over his head.

"It's pouring out," Owen said.

"I know," said Charlie. "Let's go."

"What is this?"

"It's Dad," he said. "He took his rifle into the woods."

Owen caught the look in Charlie's eyes and he did not ask anything further. A few minutes later they were out the front door, the screen slapping shut behind them, their mother moving out of the kitchen to watch them go, two boys cutting across the wet pasture on a gray, rainy fall day to find their father in the woods.

They were children of Eden and they knew these forests and hills even better than their father did. He had been taking the two of them deer hunting since they were old enough to shoot a gun. Charlie got his first spikehorn when he was eight, Owen a year later. He still remembered seeing the deer from the stand they had built, how it stood between the trees, how beautiful it was, how his father told him when to pull the trigger, how the animal collapsed to the forest floor when he did. He remembered how he cried when he stood over the carcass, the life having already seeped out of it. How his father lighted a cigarette at that moment and put his hand on the back of his neck, told him it was good to cry, it showed he respected the killing. And he remembered how he felt better when the venison was on the menu at their restaurant and his father proudly told anyone who would listen that it was Charlie's venison.

Now Owen entered the forest of tamarack, spruce, and maple first, at the only clear opening, an overgrown logging road. The boys did not speak, they figured their father would most likely have gone to the stand; it was the only logical destination. They went as fast as they could, a half run down the old logging road, stopping to climb over fallen trees. The road was narrow and led them away from the house and around the side of the ridge. The tree cover was heavy here and they could no longer feel the rain though their shirts were soaked through from the run across the wet field.

Soon the makeshift road came to an end and in front of them was the thick forest, sloping sharply away from them, some hills visible through the trees, some partially obscured by a rising mist. Their experienced eyes picked up the deer run that started to their right, little more than a break between trees, wide enough for one man to pass through. They took this and it was narrow and the forest fell away steeply on their left and the going was slow. The run led them along the spine of the hill and they knew that shortly it would intersect with another, wider run that would lead them to the stand in the large oak. They had both seen the footprints in the wet mud beneath their feet; sloshing footprints from their father's boots, though it was hard to tell how long ago he had made them.

Soon they hit a stretch where they could move quicker, the run widening a bit, when they heard it. A sound like no other, a sound they knew intimately. Its report echoed off the hills and back to them and Charlie said, "Fuck," and they began to run as fast as they could, recklessly moving downhill, their hands in front of them in case they tumbled.

They reached the intersection of the larger run and they could sprint here, side by side, their breath coming hard and fast as they went. When they reached the small clearing where the stand was, they saw it, the stand, but there was no sign of their father. They stood breathing heavily next to the tree, and with no canopy above them now the soft cool rain soaked their hair.

Charlie scanned the small meadow with his eyes and then he saw his father, and in the half-second he looked over at his brother, he knew he had seen him, too. He was directly across from them, slumped against a tree on the ground.

"Oh, Jesus," Owen said.

When they reached him, he almost looked normal, as if he had decided to stop and rest. But there was a burned smell in the air and no amount of rain could conceal the fact that the back half of their father's head was no longer there. That there was a mass of blood-matted hair and then nothing.

Charlie heard his brother's sobs and inside him there was a pain like he had never felt before. He sank to his knees. Sank to the muddy ground. There was a ringing in his ears and he became aware of the spinning of the earth beneath him. He wanted nothing more at that moment than to find something to hang on to, something to make it stop.

1

They buried Charles Bender on a cool fall day when the sun moved in and out of high clouds. They buried him in the cemetery on a sloping hill above the town of Eden, Vermont, in a cemetery with gravestones that dated back to the mid-1800s, gravestones with names barely legible, babies next to mothers, mothers next to fathers. It was where all the oldest names of Eden were: Morse, Beckett, Singleton, Fiske, Walden.

The plot Charlotte picked was near the top of the hill, near where the forest started, and from it you could see, if your eyes were good, the restaurant he had named many years ago after his wife. You could see Charlotte's itself by tracing the Dog River where it ran through the trees, where it straightened out on the stretch by the Old County Road. You could make out the roof of the former schoolhouse and you could see the river running past it and you could see where it fitted into the world around it.

From the truck in front of the gates, Charlie saw that the funeral-home people had already arrived. He saw the black hearse parked up among the stones, near their father's final resting place. Charlie was behind the wheel of the truck, his mother in the seat next to him, Owen, his brother, leaning over the bench behind. They all wore dark sunglasses. Of the two boys, Charlie was more his father's son. He was almost six feet four, as tall as Charles had been, and at eighteen years old he still had a full head of brown hair, though you could see where it was starting to recede on his forehead and where it was thinning. He had his father's pale blue eyes, a robin's egg blue, and while you might not think him handsome, there was a strength about him, a presence, that echoed his father.

By contrast, his brother, Owen, the younger by a year, had the good fortune to physically resemble his mother. Charlotte was the kind of beauty seldom seen in Eden, a tall, willowy blonde who turned heads. Owen had her fair hair, and her sharp green eyes, and he was tall, too, though not as tall as his brother, closer to six feet two, and slender. He had his mother's features, her small nose, her high cheekbones, and you might have thought him a pretty boy if it were not for the saving grace of his jaw, which suggested his father, strong and angular, and had the effect of making his whole face masculine.

The boys were waiting for their mother. They knew they were on her schedule and they were grateful for it. They were grateful for her grief for in an odd way it dulled their own. It made it possible for them to focus on something beyond what haunted them after discovering their father in the woods.

Their mother said, "Let's go."

At the graveside, the funeral director, a kind man named Crane, asked them if they wanted to say anything and they did not and nodded no and he did not respond but looked at the two men on either side of the shiny oak coffin, and while they watched, Charles Bender was lowered into the loamy earth.

Charlotte looked away when the boys fulfilled tradition by scooping out handfuls of soil and throwing them onto the shiny wood of the coffin, the granules of dirt sliding off it and running down the sides. When the men began shoveling in the hole, the three of them turned and began to walk back down the drive, Charlie and Owen, standing on either side of their mother, locking arms, as if supporting her, which they were doing, but supporting themselves as well.

THEY DROVE in the pickup down the back roads of Eden to Charlotte's. It was cold enough outside to have the heat on in the truck and it was warm as they went. The late-afternoon sun hung low and fat above the mountains. There was a light breeze and the first fallen leaves blew in front of the tires on the hard dirt road. The dirt was darkened from the heavy rain of the previous week. They did not pass any cars and Charlie drove fast. Normally Charlotte would have said something about his driving but this time she gazed blank-faced out the window to her right at the passing woods. Charlie wished someone would say something, anything, and when he thought he should, his brother shattered the silence from the back by saying, "Who's going to be here?"

Charlie saw his mother shrug. She said, "Friends of your father's. He had a lot of friends. Not close friends, of course, but people who knew him."

"Acquaintances?" Owen said.

"Something like that," his mother said. "The waitresses, of course. Probably some of the farmers."

"What do we need to do?" said Charlie.

"I don't know," Charlotte said, and then paused for a moment before saying, "Be strong."

Charlie pulled into the parking lot. It was full of cars and pickup trucks like the one they drove. When they stepped out, they could hear the soft flow of the river behind Charlotte's and they could hear a car heading their way on the road, the distinctive muted sound of tires on the hard dirt.

Together, as they had done leaving the cemetery, they walked toward the former schoolhouse, the restaurant their father had built, and they walked arm in arm, Charlotte between her two tall sons. They still wore their sunglasses and when they reached the solid wooden door that led into the dining room they did not take them off, though they paused for a moment, as if collecting their shared breath, and then Charlie moved forward and brought the latch of the handle down and pushed the door open.

The dining-room tables had been removed and the room was full of people. Most of the talking stopped when they entered and heads turned but then, as if conscious of the silence, people awkwardly picked up their conversations and tried not to stare. Charlie made out the waitresses, huddled near the bar, and he saw Joe Collins, the dishwasher, and he saw some of the regular customers and the men who brought the beef and the pork and the lamb. He saw the organic vegetable farmers, bearded men in

their thirties who relied on people like his father with their be-
liefs about food for their business. With them were women he did
not know, Vermont women with their dark hair streaked naturally with gray, women who probably taught school or did some
other work that allowed the farm to run and allowed them to have
children and keep a pottery studio out in their barn. They were
people who thought they had known his father but Charlie knew
that was not possible.

"I need a drink," said Owen.

"Ditto," said Charlie.

"Mom?" said Owen.

"Vodka," she said.

Owen left them and went to the bar. Some of the waitresses
moved toward them and they were full of condolences, and Charlie watched their lips when they talked but he barely heard what
they had to say. It had only been a few days but he was already of
the mind that there were only certain things that people could
say in situations like this and he thought he had already heard
them all. He saw his mother hugging these women, and how they
hugged her back; and his mother was the model of graciousness.
Charlotte had lived long enough to know her role and when the
situation warranted it, and Charlie was grateful when a moment
later his brother was back with their drinks, his mother's vodka
on ice and amber liquid for the two of them.

"What is it?" Charlie said.

"Bourbon," said Owen.

"Good."

Charlotte spoke first. She took one long sip of her drink and
then put it down on the windowsill. Everyone in the old
classroom-turned-dining-room faced her, and as she talked she

kept swiping at the long strands of hair that fell over her angular face. She surprised Charlie with the forthrightness of her remarks and he admired her for what she said.

She said, "I want to thank you all for being here. My husband would have really enjoyed this. All of you filling this space with drinks in your hands." She smiled. "He loved this room," and as she said this, she extended her hands outward to take it all in. "He really loved this room. I remember when he first showed it to me, and it was all run-down and he said he wanted to make it into a restaurant. I thought he was crazy." A pause, some light laughter. "But he was right, as he was about so many things. My Charles," she said, "did things his own way. He was a visionary, I think. I really do. He saw an old schoolhouse and thought that people would learn to love it as he did. And they have. I mean, look at us. How many meals have we shared together here? Here on this road next to the river. God, how he loved this place. And I want to tell you something. Charles may have done things his own way, but he did them right. There was no cutting corners with that man. He wanted the best of everything and he knew what the best was and he wanted to pass it on. To me, to his boys, and to all of you. He did that. He did. But Charles lived life on his own terms. He could be difficult, and those of you who worked for him I don't expect you to acknowledge that, not now anyway. That is not what we are here for. But he could. We all saw it. We live in a small town. When Charles brought me here from New York that was clear right away. How small this place was. How beautiful. And in a small town there are no secrets. There can't be. It's not possible. And so I want to say this. And I want my sons especially to hear it though I think they know it."

Charlotte reached out then, reached out to both Charlie and

Owen, and she put a hand on each of their shoulders and they leaned slightly into their smaller mother. She continued, "Charles died the way he chose to live. You can call it what you want. You can whisper about it however you will. And that is your right. I won't take it away—I can't take it away. But it was on his own terms. And that is all I mean to say about that."

When she finished speaking, the room was so silent you could hear when people shifted their weight from one foot to the other. First she turned to Owen and he hugged her hard, and then she turned to Charlie and he did the same. When she faced the room again, Charlie raised his glass and said, "To my father. To Charles Bender."

A roomful of people raised their glasses. The dying light slanted through the large schoolhouse windows. The restaurant had never been so crowded.

2

They moved around the farmhouse like ghosts. It had only been a few days since the boys had carried their father out of the woods. They had carried him on their backs, taking turns, and they had looked like pictures they had seen of Indian men dancing with bear carcasses on. They had looked like men carrying a huge cross.

Charlie would never forget the feeling of his father on his back. And he would never forget seeing his mother on the porch as she waited for them and seeing in her eyes that she knew that this was what they would find. For a moment he filled with anger for her, for why would she send her boys into the forest if she knew that this was what awaited them. But Charlie also realized that his anger was as useless as this incessant rain in the fall.

After they had laid their father on the porch and Owen had gone inside to make the call, he went to his mother and took her in his arms and he held her. She was sobbing so hard she was having trouble breathing and he wanted desperately for her to be strong, but he understood that this was not possible. He wanted to hold her until she could not cry anymore. Her tears were wet on his shoulder and she seemed small in his arms. He held her tight. "It's okay," he said. "It's okay." He said it over and over and he wanted to believe it.

Now, with only the three of them, the house felt empty. Charlotte took to the bedroom, coming down to throw a dinner together which she barely ate herself, returning upstairs with a large glass of vodka and disappearing until the next morning. Owen spent all his time with his pretty girlfriend, Claire Apple, driving off in her father's station wagon. They offered to take Charlie with them, but because he did not want to be a third wheel and because he wanted to be alone, he instead spent much of his time out in the barn, sitting on the edge of the hayloft, looking across the hills and thinking about his father.

The night before he took his life, Charles Bender had closed Charlotte's for the first time since Owen was born. He had called Charlie and Owen at home and told them not to bother coming in. They did not question him, for he was a man who had never invited questioning from his children. And so while Charlie said nothing, it worried him since he knew what his brother and his mother knew and that none of them had been willing to say out loud: his father was dying.

The truth was that Charles Bender, since the time he was twelve, had loved cigarettes. He loved to smoke. He loved everything about it. He loved the feel of the thin cigarette in his

hands, the inhaling of the smoke into his lungs, the contempla-
tive mood that smoking put him in. He especially loved smoking
at the end of a busy night, preferably in the summer when it was
warm, when he could sit on the back porch of Charlotte's and listen to the clink of dishes being washed, dishes on which he had
delivered the best food he could deliver; and listen, too, to the
river and the woods and know that the day behind him was a day
richly lived.

About six months before the night he closed the restaurant,
though, Charles had developed a persistent cough. A cough that
started low in his chest and in the mornings was especially bad;
a hack that hurt him more than he let on. One morning in the
spring, he had coughed so hard that he broke a rib, though he
did not tell anyone. Charlie came out the back of Charlotte's and
found his father sitting on the steps, half bent over, clutching his
side. When he saw his son, Charles said, "I'm okay."

"You sure?" said Charlie.

His father nodded. "Get back inside."

And Charlie did as he was told, though he went right to the
dining room where his mother was, where she stood looking over
that evening's reservations. He told her what he had seen and he
said, "He needs to go to a doctor."

"You know your father."

"We should do something."

The boy watched his mother sigh, look at him for a moment,
then take her hand and run it through his brown hair. "He won't
do it, Charlie, you know that. He's a stubborn man and he hates
doctors."

They went on and they did not speak of it again. Then their father closed the restaurant, and that night in the kitchen of the

farmhouse, he cooked for them as a family. The sons, who had worked in the restaurant since they were small children, knew this was no ordinary meal. They watched their father grill oysters until they had just opened, and then drop the smallest amount of his best veal reduction onto the shellfish, saying to Charlotte and the boys as they sampled them, "Taste the salt, the sea."

They watched him sear the duck confit he had made himself and hung in the barn. They watched him shred the meat off the bone and use it in a salad of dandelion greens and dried cranberries, drizzling a warm ginger vinaigrette over all of it.

They opened bottle after bottle of wine from the part of the cellar they were not to touch. And by the time they had finished a chateaubriand, the meat sliced thin and sauced with Madeira and wild morels, they were getting drunk from the wine and they knew it was the best meal they had ever had and they would probably never have one better.

Later, while Owen and Charlie cleaned up, their parents danced in the living room to an Etta James record. It was something they used to do, when the boys were small. Through the kitchen door he saw his father dip his mother down, bring her back up, and then they moved off and out of sight together. He did not know what tomorrow would bring. But for the first time in a while, that night they felt like a normal family, people who didn't just work together but ate together, danced together, talked together, told the archetypal stories that all families have. Sitting in the barn loft in the days after his father's suicide, Charlie thought of this the most. That dinner. His parents dancing. The sound of his mother's laughter as his father swung her around.

That night when he returned, Owen joined Charlie in the hayloft. From where he sat, Charlie had seen Claire Apple's car come up the driveway, stop for a moment, and then its headlights as it retreated through the trees and back down the hill. Owen knew where to find him, and when he came up the rickety stairs and into the loft they sat with their legs dangling out the wide doors and the night was bright and star-filled. Owen held out his hand.

"I brought you a joint," he said.

"Thanks," said Charlie, though he didn't take it.

Owen moistened one end of the joint with his lips and then lit the other end. He inhaled and passed it along to his brother, who drew on it.

"What'd you guys do?" Charlie asked.

"Drove around mostly. Ended up at the lake. There were a few people. Drank some beer. Nothing much."

"How's Claire?"

"She's good. She doesn't understand why you won't come with us."

Charlie took another hit off the joint and shrugged. "I don't know."

"It's not a big deal."

"I know. I just felt like being here."

"Did Mom tell you Sam is coming tomorrow?"

"Uncle Sam?"

"Yeah. She didn't? He is."

"Tomorrow?"

"Yeah."

"What for?"

"What else? It's about Dad."

Charlie looked across the hills to the dark mountains. "I guess that makes sense."

"Think he's going to ask about the restaurant?"

"I don't know," said Charlie.

"Me neither," Owen said. "Mom didn't say."

"Well, she's barely there."

"I know. I don't think she left her room all day."

In the distance they heard the sound of a truck shifting through the switchbacks on nearby Spruce Mountain. They relaxed into the high. They smoked the joint until it was nothing more than a tiny nub that began to burn their fingertips. Owen took the roach and stashed it with the others on a rafter behind the door. When he sat down again he leaned back on his elbows and said "Yep," and they both laughed at this like it was the funniest thing they had ever heard. Then they sat again in silence. They were brothers and they knew each other better than they had ever known anybody, and when you are like this you can sit in silence and not speak and it is the most comfortable thing in the world.

3

Uncle Sam was Sam Marsh and he was not an uncle at all but their father's oldest friend. More than anyone else, he was responsible for Eden, and for Charlotte's.

In the fall of 1962, two years before Charlie was born, Charles and Charlotte Bender were newly married and living in New York City. Charles had come from the upper peninsula of Michigan and had always loved the outdoors. He had grown up hunting and fishing. He had gone to the city for college and this was where he met Charlotte. Charlotte had studied to become a teacher and finished school, but college was not for Charles and he dropped out. He began to work in restaurants and she taught kindergarten, and in their neighborhood they ran with a group of artists and theater people and on many nights they would enter-

tain them at their small apartment, Charles cooking for everyone. Nights when they stayed up late and drank and smoked and
talked about art and poetry and food. It was a heady time and
they were young and in love and for Charlotte there was no place
she wanted to be more than the city, with its colorful people and
busy streets. For Charles, though, there was always something
missing, and until he joined a few of his friends on a hunting trip
to northern Vermont he did not know exactly what it was.

Sam Marsh had a deer camp on the fringe of Eden, Vermont,
and the moment Charles saw this small northern town, with its
views of the mountains and its rolling highlands, he knew what
had been missing from his life.

On the second day of his trip, they were driving down the Old
County Road when Charles noticed the abandoned schoolhouse
next to the river. Stuck in the grass by the road was a simple sign
that read: FOR SALE BY OWNER.

Charles turned to Sam Marsh and said, "Stop."

They pulled over, and much to Sam's annoyance spent two
hours walking around the land, looking into the windows of the
run-down old school building, staring down the steep valley toward Hunger Mountain. It was a beautiful fall day, peak foliage,
and the grass of the floodplain was the brightest of greens. Later
Charles would say that a gentle calm had come over him, and he
knew that he was home.

That afternoon he called the number on the sign and without
consulting Charlotte or anyone else he bought the place on the
spot for a song. "What are you going to do with it?" Sam Marsh
asked him.

"Live here," said Charles.

They hunted for two more days and they did not get any deer

but for Charles that was okay. There would be lots of time for deer hunting. On their return trip he phoned Charlotte from a pay phone at a gas station and he told her that he had bought an old schoolhouse, in the most enchanting place he had ever seen, on the edge of a river with views of the hills and the mountains and no other houses visible from it. He told her to start packing, that while the weather was still warm he wanted to move and begin renovations right away. It will take some work, he said, but this is where we are meant to be.

When Charlotte caught her breath she said, "You're lucky I don't divorce you right now."

The following week Charlotte and Charles arrived back in Eden and when she saw the schoolhouse she did not see the beauty that Charles saw; she did not feel its magic the way he did; she did not fall in love with the river and the hills full of color. She cried. She tried to stop but she could not and as much as he hoped they were tears of joy he knew her well enough to know better. "What the hell am I going to do here?" she said. "Tell me that. There is nothing for me here."

"I'm here, Charlotte," he told her. "That should be enough."

They stayed that night at the inn at Eden and they ate dinner in its wood-paneled restaurant. Over a bottle of wine they could hardly afford, Charles made his case for the move. He told her they could build a life here richer than any they could have in the city. He said that she should just watch: their friends from the city would realize the wisdom of their decision and follow them. He talked about the cost of living, and anything else he could think of. Finally he told her about what it would be like for their children to grow up in the safe, majestic woods, building forts among the trees, skipping over stone walls, swimming in the river on summer afternoons. He cajoled and he pleaded and she said nothing until later when they lay together and then she conceded he was probably right about the children. She said, "I'll move here with you, but not to that schoolhouse."

And so they found the farmhouse on Signal Ridge. It, too, was run-down, and had belonged to a bachelor in his nineties who had died there, but it was large and cheap and had land with views. They had to buy it full of the old man's belongings, and they spent the first several weeks there cleaning it out, tending to a large bonfire in the yard. Now that the decision was made to be in Eden, Charlotte threw herself into the work of making house and this pleased Charles greatly, and many of their friends from New York made the journey and helped them out.

One Saturday night in early October when much of the gang from the city had made the trip to help them put a coat of paint on the weathered clapboards, they had finished dinner and were sitting on the porch and the men smoked. They looked out at the last vestiges of sun in the sky, streaks of purple above the hills. Charlotte brought up the fact that Charles still had to sell the schoolhouse. She had found a teaching job and they could live on it for now but could not afford both places.

She said, "I'm afraid we're stuck with that elephant."

Sam Marsh said, "Why not keep it?"

"And do what?" Charlotte said.

"Open a restaurant."

Initially this elicited laughter from everyone on the porch, but as they began to talk, Charles began to see it, how it would work, and they stayed up until three in the morning talking about little else, and Charlotte gave Sam a hard time for suggesting it, but in her husband's eyes she saw the fire of certainty she had seen that night at the inn. And she knew not to get in the way of this, that it was something he needed to do. And when, a year later, the schoolhouse had been repainted, and a kitchen had been built on the back, and he showed her the handmade sign with her name in large script, she knew that this was why Charles brought her here, why they had come to Vermont, and that sometimes if you put yourself in a position to know something it comes along and reveals itself to you.

Now, almost twenty years after that day, Sam Marsh sat in a wing-backed chair in the living room of the farmhouse and looked across to Owen and Charlie on the couch. Charlotte had come downstairs and she sat on a wooden chair to the right of Sam. Sam was a big man and he filled the antique chair. He had a broad friendly face and his hair was almost entirely gray.

"I'm so sorry, guys," he said, looking at the boys. "No one loved your father more than I did."

Charlie nodded. "We know."

"Your father was something. There aren't many like him in the world. He was bullheaded, that's for sure. And I know he was tough on you. That's how he thought things should be done. How his father did things. But he loved you guys, he did. He always told me that. How proud he was."

"Thanks," said Owen.

Sam sighed. He ran one hand through his thick hair. "This is hard," he said.

"This is what he wanted, Sam," Charlotte said.

"I know."

"What?" said Charlie.

Sam looked away toward the windows and then back again. He reached into the pocket of his coat and took out an envelope.

From where Charlie sat it looked like it had no markings. Sam fingered it for a moment and then he opened it. He took out one thin piece of paper.

"Your father asked me to read this. After he was gone."

"Wait a minute," Owen said. "You knew what he was going to do?"

Sam nodded. "Yes."

"Why didn't you do anything?" Owen shouted.

"Owen," said Charlotte.

"He's right," Sam said. "I tried. I tried to talk to him. So did your mother—"

"You knew about this, too?" said Owen.

"I knew it," Charlie said. "I knew when I saw your face. On the porch."

"Guys, guys," Sam said. "Please. You have a right to be angry. Be angry at me. Not your mother. You knew your father. You knew him better than anybody. He was really sick. He didn't have long. It was a matter of weeks, not months. He didn't want to be in a hospital. He wanted to control how it ended."

"He wanted to control everything," said Owen.

"Yes, he did," Sam said. "That was your father."

"The letter," Charlie said.

Sam looked over at Charlotte. She nodded and then looked at her lap. Sam unfolded the piece of paper and began to read.

To my family. I was a lucky man. To live in a place like this. To be blessed with a wonderful wife and two strong boys. To be able to do what I loved more than anything. You heard me say it a million times, but there is nothing more important than a good meal. There is nothing more important than honoring the land and the water that gives us our food. Growing up in a restaurant is a hard life. We never had a lot of money. Everything went back into the business. To my boys, you had to work when other kids got to play. I demanded a lot from you. I know that I was a pain in the ass and there were times when you hated me. Sometimes we fought and that is part of being fathers and sons. I hope you choose to remember the good times we had. Deer hunting in the fall. Foraging for mushrooms. The trips to the ocean. There were many good times. Too many to recount here.

I want you to know that I was proud of you. Both of you. I may not have expressed it always, but I was. You were fine sons. Every father should be so lucky.

Now is the hard part. The future. I have given this a lot of thought. I have debated with myself what should happen with Charlotte's. Decisions like this are never easy but I am confident this is the right one.

I am leaving Charlotte's to Charlie. Charlie, you have the right instincts and temperament to be a good, and maybe even a great, chef. You are the right steward for Charlotte's and it is important to me that this work be continued. And since you will need a place to live, I am also leaving you the house.

As for Owen, I think it is important for you to follow your own path. As I did. You will need to discover for yourself what that is. But I know it's not here. I know it's not Eden. We had hoped that both of you would go to

college. Since neither of you has shown any interest, I am
giving ten thousand dollars of those savings to Owen. This
is a start and should help you find a new place to live.

The remainder of the savings goes to my wife. I wish it
was more. But money was never the most important thing
for us, was it? It should be enough to set you up for what's
next. As we talked about, this means New York. The city
never left you. You never loved Eden the way I did but you
sacrificed for me, for the restaurant and the boys. I hope
you love it as much as you did when we were young.

To all of you, good-bye. With love, Charles.

When Sam Marsh finished reading, he carefully refolded the
thin letter and held it in his hands. The four of them sat in silence. Charlie was stunned. He had simply figured that the three
of them would somehow try to make it work, he and Owen in the
kitchen and their mother running the front end. It never occurred to him that his father would leave it all to him. He looked
over at Owen. He saw his brother steel himself and he knew this
hurt him.

Owen spoke first. "Well, there you have it," he said.

"It's bullshit," Charlie said. "We don't have to do any of it."

"It's what it is," said Owen.

"Uncle Sam, Mom, come on," Charlie said, and he knew he
was going to cry but he could not help it. "We don't have to do
what he says, do we?"

"Charlie," Sam said.

"Don't," said Charlotte, reaching out and placing her hand on
Sam's wrist. "It's what he wanted, Charlie."

"So what about what we want?" said Charlie, and the tears were coming now and he did not care. "What about that?"

"It didn't matter when he was alive," said Owen. "It shouldn't matter now."

Owen stood then and Charlie said, "Wait," but his brother shook him off.

"I want to be alone," Owen said.

He went to the front door and no one tried to stop him. He opened it and stepped out, closing it behind him. Through the window Charlie saw him climb into the pickup truck. A moment later he heard it drive away.

4

One of Charlie's earliest memories was of his father slaughtering chickens on the floodplain behind Charlotte's. His father bought the chickens alive since they were cheaper that way, and fresher, and he'd spend an entire morning killing bird after bird and then cleaning them. Charlie remembered how his father looked then, a cap cocked on his head, a cigarette dangling from his lips. He was tall and strong, and when he raised the ax over his head, a chicken's neck pressed down flat against a tree stump with his boot, Charlie held his breath. He remembered the ax coming down, the head rolling off the chicken, and then the comical dance of death that the bird did before it succumbed, collapsing to the ground like an empty paper bag. It scared the hell out of Charlie to watch it but he couldn't turn away. He was in awe of his father and he wanted nothing more than to be at the restaurant, to watch him work.

By the time he was ten, both he and Owen were helping with the basics of prep. Peeling potatoes, chopping onions. They washed pots and pans and they were young enough that it didn't feel like labor. Their father said he liked having them around, in the room he said he loved like no other. It was a big kitchen for a small restaurant. A giant commercial stove and upright grill dominated one wall. A large wooden table in the middle. A walk-in fridge on the other side, next to a large pantry closet. Windows that looked out to the floodplain to where the Dog River snaked through the trees.

Once during dinner service his father was working the grill and Charlie and Owen were at the wooden table, sitting on stools, cleaning mushrooms with brushes. Charlie noticed that a large pot on the stove was starting to boil over with water. Instead of calling out to his father, he went to it, stood under it and was about to try to turn it down, when he was met with the open palm of his father's large hand across his face.

"Never near the stove," his father said. "Never."

The hand was gone but the sting seemed to grow and Charlie brought his own hands to his face and started to cry. Unlike when he cried over the deer he had shot, his father offered no reassuring words. Charles turned his back on him and returned to the grill.

But it was during this time, as well, that Charlotte's began to develop a reputation that belied both its size and its location. One summer a food writer from the *New York Times* was staying on the lake in nearby Greensboro when he heard about the restaurant. He came down and ate and after, when he identified himself, Charles showed him the kitchen, and allowed him to watch while he prepared a native trout.

"The last thing you want to do," Charles told the reporter, "is take a piece of fish like this and fuck it up. This thing has been out of the brook for less than twenty-four hours. If you dress it too much it will no longer taste like fish."

Charles pan-seared the fish with pancetta and lemon and served it on wild asparagus. In the newspaper the following Sunday, the reporter proclaimed that most New York chefs could learn a lot from Charles Bender of Eden, Vermont. Just like that, tiny Charlotte's became a food destination.

Not that it made much of a difference to Charles. The place was going to be full either way. It did not matter to him whether patrons were from Vermont or from New York or Boston, as long as they came. The city people might spend more on wine, which helped, but with only twenty-two seats, Charlotte's was not going to make anyone rich.

For a time, especially with the boys getting older and taking larger roles in the kitchen, he thought about expansion, about building an addition onto the back of the restaurant. But he knew that part of the reason Charlotte's worked was its size. He could focus on the best ingredients, on cooking precisely what he wanted to cook every day, and nothing more. The three or four appetizers and the six to eight entrées he had Charlotte, with her careful script, list on the blackboard, a remnant of the schoolhouse, every morning. This was his vision and he was very particular about how it was carried out.

When the boys got into their teens, Charles started teaching them to cook. They didn't ask to learn and he didn't ask them if they wanted to. It was an extension of what they had done already.

In the mornings before the rush of the day started, he gave them what he called blind baskets. On the wooden table when they arrived were straw baskets covered with a towel. Owen got one and Charlie got one. Inside each was an identical set of ingredients. One morning they might contain a whole chicken, dried porcini mushrooms, a pint of heavy cream. Another morning they might find a bowl of littleneck clams, two fresh tomatoes, and a hot pepper. Then the clock started. Working at either end of the table, and using anything they could find in the pantry, they had one hour to create a dish from what was in front of them.

They knew they were in competition with each other. Each day, Charles chose one dish over another. More often than not, Charlie won. Owen worked just as hard, but Charlie had the same gift his father had. He could see the dish in front of him before he built it. He could see the road map that led from raw ingredients to something approaching art on the plate.

The winner each day got to work the line that night. The loser had to scrub pots and pans with Joe Collins and clean the toilets. What neither of them realized at the time was that they were playing for larger stakes. This would not become apparent until later, when Sam Marsh read Charles Bender's letter in the living room of the farmhouse. All along, their father had been choosing his successor. He had been ensuring his legacy.

5

Charlotte left Eden first. In the morning when Charlie came downstairs she sat at the kitchen table with her coffee. She wore a black jacket with her jeans and her hair was tied up. Next to her were four suitcases, stacked on top of one another.

"Do you need to do this?" Charlie asked.

"I do," she said.

"You're going to New York?"

"Yes. I have friends there. I know it. It's comfortable to me. It's not like it's the other side of the earth. It's what, five, six hours? You can come see me."

"I have a restaurant to run apparently."

"Sit with me for a minute," Charlotte said.

Charlie poured himself a cup of coffee from the pot on the counter and sat across from his mother.

"I know this is hard for you, Charlie."

"Mom, please," Charlie said.

"I mean it. Listen to me. I know this is hard. It's hard on all of us. But this is the right thing, Charlie. You are going to do great at the restaurant. I know you will. You were born to it."

"I don't care about that."

"You don't now. But in time you will. Trust me."

Charlie looked away. He didn't feel like talking about this anymore. "You have a train to catch," he said.

"Wake your brother," said Charlotte. "You can both take me."

THEY DROVE their mother to Montpelier on a clear fall day to catch the train to New York City. Charlotte sat in back, Charlie drove, and Owen sat next to him. When they reached the train station they stood on the platform and looked through the cut in the woods where the nose of the train would show itself. When the breeze blew it suggested the winter to come and Charlotte brought her arms to her chest to guard against it.

"This I won't miss," she said, and she laughed slightly and no one laughed with her.

"You'll call?" Charlie asked.

"Of course," she said. "As soon as I get settled. Until then, you can get me through Sam. Anytime."

They heard the train before they saw it, a low rumble through the trees and then the horn when it reached a crossing. Soon it came around the bend and it slowed, passing them before coming to a halt. The doors opened and a few people got off.

"Hugs," Charlotte said. "No tears."

Charlie held her first and then Owen. He watched them embrace and he knew his brother was next. That it would just be him and a restaurant on the river.

"I love you both," Charlotte said, after the hugs. She stood in front of them and she looked small to Charlie. He knew she was going to defy her own edict and cry and she did, her eyes growing wet. "My two boys," she said.

"You're going to miss the train, Mom," said Owen.

"They'll wait for me," said Charlotte.

She came to them and they both put an arm around her and her face for a moment fell into Charlie's chest.

"Soon," she said.

"Soon," said Charlie.

They picked up her bags and helped her to the steps where the young steward took the suitcases from them, one by one, hoisting them up and into the car. A moment later they saw her in the fifth window down, where she blew them a kiss. They waved. The train sat for what seemed a long time, before slowly pulling away from the depot. Charlotte faced forward and they saw her in profile. They watched her until they could not see her anymore. The train picked up speed and sounded its horn as it entered the trees.

6

On the ride home, Charlie made his pitch to Owen. They were cutting through the forest on Route 15, most of the trees here already bare, and the road followed a pebbly bottomed stream. Charlie said, "You don't have to leave."

"What am I going to do?"

"Stay here. Run the restaurant with me."

"That wasn't his plan," said Owen.

"So what? It's just us now. We don't have to do it."

"I know. But it won't work. It never does. Sooner or later it'll just fuck us up. When you get money involved, that's what happens. That's why he always said he would never have a partner."

"It's different, Owen. It's us. You know that."

"Nah, it's not. He screwed me. And that's the way it is."

"He screwed you?"

"Of course. I mean, look at it. You got a restaurant, valued at what? Two hundred, three hundred thousand? And a house and forty acres, no mortgage. Another three hundred thousand? What'd I get? Ten grand and the boot."

Charlie sighed. He steered through an S curve, taking it slower than he normally did. In front of him a logging truck crossed the centerline as it made the sharp turn. There was no oncoming traffic and they were back on a straightaway. "I would split it all with you right now. I would."

"I appreciate that," said Owen. "And I believe you. I do. But I couldn't live with it. You can understand that, right?"

"Yeah, I guess."

"I know why he did it, too."

"What do you mean?"

"Montreal."

"No," said Charlie, though he knew in the shorthand brothers use what Owen meant. Two years ago Owen had skipped off to Montreal with some friends when he was supposed to be at the restaurant because they could get into bars there. It was a busy Saturday night and Owen tried to talk Charlie into going but he wouldn't. "Go tomorrow," Charlie told him, but Owen had made up his mind. Charlie knew their father would blow up and he did, staying up most of the night smoking on the porch and waiting for Owen to return. When the car dropped Owen off at the house in the morning, Charlie wished there was some way he could warn him. He lay in bed and knew what was going to happen. Owen opened the door and Charles was right inside it, and before Owen could say anything, his father struck him on the side of the head with his closed fist. When Owen grabbed his head and folded over, his father said, "Take care of your obligations."

And he didn't say anything else about it, and Owen didn't either. Later that same day Owen worked at Charlotte's as if nothing had happened.

"I'm telling you," said Owen. "He never forgave me for that."

Charlie nodded. "It was pretty stupid."

"Yeah," said Owen. "It was. I should've punched him back."

OWEN STAYED in Eden for three more nights. He spent most of his time in what had been their parents' bedroom with Claire Apple. Charlie gave them their space, retreating to the restaurant, cleaning out the walk-in of meat and produce that had gone bad in the time they had been closed. Though at night he heard them talking through the walls, and sometimes he heard them making love though he tried not to listen to this. Charlie had only been with one woman, and that was in a windowless building across the border in Quebec. It was a strip club that he and Owen and a few other guys from school drove to with the express purpose of losing their virginity. The prostitute had dirty blond hair and was a little heavy, and she spoke no English, which Charlie was happy about. It took the pressure off him, and when she put a condom on him with her mouth, he closed his eyes and then she was on top of him and it was over quickly.

Eden was so small that it was difficult, unless you were Owen, to find a girlfriend. Charlie's high school, which he had left the year before without graduating, had only twenty-six students in his class and fewer than seventy in the entire school. Charlie

wasn't even sure how it started with Claire. About six months before Owen had told Charlie about some party out in a field and
said he had their ride covered. Claire Apple picked them up.
Charlie knew who she was, though Charlie had only spoken to
her a few times. In the car Owen held her hand while she drove.
Charlie had known she was pretty but now that he had gotten
close to her he realized how true that was. She had black hair
that fell in curls to her shoulders. Fair, clear skin. Eyes so big
and dark they seemed to have no white. A slightly long face and
a petite nose, full lips. She did not wear makeup and she did not
need to. She was not slender but ran more to curvy. Most of all,
she didn't act like she knew she was pretty. She had a nice way
about her and she treated Charlie right away not like Owen's
brother, but like a friend, and he liked her for this. This alone
made her different from the other girlfriends Owen had had.

Now Charlie wondered what would happen to the two of them
after Owen left. Owen hadn't said anything, though Charlie
knew Claire had another year of school. She was a good student
and her father ran the local bank. They had money. She could
go to any college she wanted, Owen had said. She was not long
for Eden either.

THE MORNING Owen left Charlie watched his brother and Claire
from the kitchen window as they said good-bye. They hugged for
a long time, leaning against her father's Volvo, and when they
pulled apart Charlie saw that she had been crying hard and his
heart went out to her. Owen stayed in the driveway until her car

disappeared down the drive and then he came into the kitchen. Charlie had moved to the table so that Owen wouldn't know he had been watching.

"That was hard," Owen said.

"She okay?"

"She'll be fine."

Charlie nodded. "She's nice. Claire."

"I know. She's a good one. She's going to come see me." Owen looked at the clock above the stove. "I didn't realize it was so late. My bus leaves at eleven."

Charlie stood. "Let me get my coat."

And for the second time that week Charlie drove to Montpelier to drop off someone he loved without knowing when he would see them next. Once in the truck they rode in silence. As soon as they reached the main road it started to rain. They watched the wipers and the road and Charlie thought he should say something but he knew he had done all he could to try to get Owen not to leave. Owen had made up his mind and Charlie knew his brother well enough to know what that meant. He was on his way to Boston today and then hopefully, he said, the Cape. He had always loved the ocean.

When they reached the bus station, little more than a white trailer next to the railroad tracks, the bus had not yet arrived. They stood outside and kept their hands in their pockets against the cold. In front of them they could see the golden dome of the statehouse and behind it a hill full of leafless trees rose up against the dark sky. Standing there, they fell into a familiar rhythm, as if there was nothing odd about this. They small-talked about the restaurant, about the winter to come. They talked as if this were some weekend trip Owen was about to take, as if in a few days they would stand in this same place before getting back into the truck for the drive to Eden.

In time the bus pulled in and passengers stepped out into the cold and waited for the driver to open the side compartments so they could get their bags.

"Well, this is it," Owen said, reaching down for his duffel bag.

"Please let me know where you are," said Charlie.

Owen nodded. Charlie saw that his eyes were moist but he did not say anything about it. This is hard on him, too, he thought. He just does not want me to know it.

"All right," said Charlie.

And they embraced then, awkwardly, the embrace of siblings at a parting, Charlie patting Owen on the back as he held him. Charlie wanted to cry at the uncertainty of it all but he did not want his brother to see this. Instead, when they pulled away from each other, he gave him a big smile, touched his shoulder for a moment. Owen returned the smile and then turned away from Charlie, handed his ticket to the driver, and walked up the steps into the bus.

Charlie waited until the bus pulled out of the parking lot and turned left across the river and over the iron trestle bridge. He watched the bus move toward the highway until he lost sight of it behind a large brick building. Then he climbed back into the cab of his truck and drove back to Eden, back to an empty house.

7

The son now stood in place of the father. That winter Charlie gave himself completely to the restaurant, arriving in the morning when it was still dark, leaving after midnight. During dinner service he was like a man possessed, sauces bubbling on the stoves, fish searing in hot pans, meats needing to be turned at precise intervals on the grill. In truth, it was too much work now for one; unlike his father, he did not have two boys who could help.

But Charlie loved the cooking, loved the heat of the moment when six entrées were going at once on the line, when the waitresses could not hustle the food out fast enough for his liking.

Most nights he was so bone-tired that back at the farmhouse on Signal Ridge pouring himself a glass of brandy was nothing more than a ritual: he would barely have a sip before he was snoring in the large armchair in front of the television. Sometimes he would spend the entire night here, and other times he would wake in the deep blue of early morning and struggle upstairs to his bed.

Sundays, the only day the restaurant was closed, were hard for him now. Before, when his father was alive, he looked forward to Sundays, a time when he would not have to work. Now he wandered around the house, wondering what to do with himself. He realized, with Owen gone, that most of his social life, such as it was, had come through Owen. He had never made much of an effort to reach out because he didn't have to. Owen had brought friends into their lives. Now when he ran into friends he knew from high school who had not left town, he always promised to meet them for a drink, to give a call, but he knew he would not and they seemed to understand this as well and didn't hold him to it.

And on those quiet Sunday afternoons he began to take long walks. Regardless of the weather, he would put on his boots and head out the driveway to the miles of dirt road that cut through the woods of Eden. Sometimes he walked through heavy snow, under the limbs of the evergreens that leaned over the road. Other times the brilliant sunshine in the winter sky almost blinded him with its reflection off the snowy fields. At any rate Charlie trudged along until it tired him out, and then he returned home to the woodstove and to a simple dinner he made for himself, the one night he did not cook for others.

But mostly, he worked.

One afternoon at Charlotte's he decided to clean out the old pantry and he was hard at it when he heard laughter from just out the porch door, where Althea and Peg, the two waitresses who had been there since the beginning, were smoking cigarettes. It was a job that had not been done in ages, and there were jars of spices as old he was. He was standing on a stool, rifling through old boxes, when he heard their laughter and it occurred to him that it might be directed toward him. He got off the stool, went to the door, looked at the two older women smoking in the cold, put his hands on his hips, and with mock anger said, "What?"

"Honey," Althea said in her roughened voice. "You need to get laid."

And when she said it, the two women broke into peals of laughter, and Charlie couldn't help but laugh himself.

"What makes you think I'm not—" he began to say.

"You don't have time," Althea said. "You never leave here. If you were getting laid, trust me, we'd know about it."

"That's nice," Charlie said. "That's really nice."

And then he went back inside and he could hear them laughing and he knew it was good-natured and meant to be, but that when you got right down to it, they were right. He needed a woman. But this was Eden, and that was easier said than done. Most of the girls he knew had left for college and it was not like he was in a position to meet people, unless they came into the restaurant on one of those infrequent occasions when he ventured out front, or he hired them to wait tables, which would require one of the waitresses who had been there since the beginning to leave. Charlie knew this was unlikely, and he did not dwell on it, though somewhere within he understood that there was something missing from his life, and he did not yet know how to find it.

————

ONCE A month, on a Sunday evening when he was home, Charlie heard from his mother. She called him around dinnertime and they would usually talk for close to an hour. He told her about the restaurant and about the house and she always acted as if nothing interested her more. As he talked, though, he sensed her distance. He could not help but tell her about his life for she was his mother and the life was his, regardless of the fact that it was a world she had left behind, almost as if it never happened, as if she had never come from New York all those years ago with a man who had a dream she believed in. The truth was they were much more comfortable when they talked about her life. How she was enjoying the city; all her old friends in the Village who had her over for dinner; what it was like to walk down those tree-lined streets in winter. So different from Eden, she said. People everywhere, people from all over the world. And the food, Charlie, she told him, the food. Your father, she said, loved Eden because he could cook what came from the land and the rivers around him. And she understood that. But, she told Charlie, New York by comparison is the world's supermarket. You would not believe what you can find here.

For his part, Charlie listened carefully to what she had to say. But he was his father's son and what she told him had little appeal: it was not something he thought about ever as something that might apply to him. New York might as well have been Hong Kong. Sure, he was too young to be set in his ways, but Eden was what he knew and he figured that it was all he would ever know. And he thought this was the way it should be.

While Charlie talked to his mother once a month, a winter

passed with no word from Owen. Charlotte was aware, of course, of Owen's departure and sometimes they speculated about it and where he was, and often when it was discussed they were reduced to clichés, the "no news is good news" refrain.

One day Charlie was at the post office, and when he turned around from the counter, he found Claire Apple next in line looking down at what she was about to mail.

"Claire," he said.

She looked up and smiled. "Hi, Charlie," she said.

"How are you?"

She shrugged. "Okay, I guess. For winter." She laughed. "Have you heard from Owen?"

"No," he said, "I was going to ask you that."

Claire shook her head. "He said he was going to call me when he got to Boston but I never heard from him."

"I'm sorry."

"It's all right. I was really angry and hurt for a while but it's probably for the best. That's what my mother says. But what does she know? Anyway, it looks like I'll be in Chicago next year."

"Chicago?"

"Northwestern. I got in early acceptance."

"Congratulations, Claire. That's great."

"Thanks, Charlie. It's something, right?"

"Yeah. It really is."

"It was nice to see you."

"You, too," Charlie said. "And good luck."

And she smiled once more at him, and for the first time he noticed how her cheeks dimpled. His brother was a fool for not having called her, he thought. Maybe there were lots of girls like Claire in the world but Charlie doubted it.

———

IN LATE March of that year, the first signs of spring reached Eden. This was Charlie's favorite time. The days were getting longer, the summer still to come, the year long and in front of him and full of promise. Winter now squarely at his back. Some nights at the restaurant it was warm enough to open the windows and the soft breeze moved through the kitchen and the dining room, and when there was a break in the clatter of the kitchen he could hear the peepers in the marsh, the steady breathing of the woods. New life all around him and this was Eden and you could not help but feel it.

In the morning, as his father had taught him to, he foraged in the woods near the river for the wild ramps that grew for only a few short weeks. At Charlotte's he threw them on the grill with a touch of olive oil, salt, and pepper and their oniony flavor was the perfect accompaniment for grilled meats. He also stopped on the sides of the road and amid the early ferns he found the first fiddleheads of the season and these he deep-fried as a side dish. There were also the wild mushrooms of the year, chanterelles and oysters and pheasants. He harvested them on long hikes in the woods and turned them into stocks and stuffing and roasted them with pine nuts, garlic, and rosemary. He smothered the spring lamb raised by a farmer out in Glover with their woody flavor.

One sunny morning Charlie checked the mail in the box out by the road at the farmhouse on Signal Ridge. In addition to the usual bills and catalogs, there was also a postcard. He felt his heart leap in his chest. Before he even had a chance to absorb the picture on the front, which showed a city from the air, with

the word *Rio* written in broad script across the photo, he knew
who it was from. He turned it over. There was the familiar handwriting of his younger brother and it told him what he wanted to
know. Owen had joined the Merchant Marines and was working
as a chef on a freighter. "Cooking sloppy joes, if you can believe
it," he wrote. "The ocean is endless, blue forever, but the sunsets
are the coolest thing you've ever seen. The ports are nice. Three
months at sea, three off. Owen."

Charlie stood there with the woods all around him and read
the postcard over and over. His hand shook slightly and after the
third time he began to laugh out loud.

They came at three- and four-month intervals for the next five
years. From all over the world. Panama. The Azores. Corsica.
London. Rotterdam. Places that Charlie could scarcely imagine,
though in his mind he often pictured his handsome brother
walking the streets of strange cities teeming with people, eating
in small cafés, sleeping in motels where the sound of foreign
voices reached his room. They were two brothers separated now
by the size of the world and its broad expanse of oceans. But they
were fulfilling the prophecies that had been handed to them,
handed to them in the woods of Eden on a fall day when the rain
fell in torrents and wiped away much of what they had come to
rely on, to believe in.

8

They say that different people deal with the passing of time differently. In Eden, Vermont, for instance, it is a commonly shared belief that time can be slowed if you live deliberately. If you stop and watch sunsets. If you spend time sitting on porches listening to the woods. If you give in to the reality of the seasons. And the two other seasons that are noted here: stick season, the time when the leaves are off the trees and the snow has not yet arrived. And, of course, mud season, arriving in late March or early April, when the dirt roads give up a winter's worth of ice pack and driving becomes nearly impossible, the roads full of deep grooves and, in places, soft as quicksand.

Charlie Bender, like his father before him, loved Eden and its woods and valleys and rivers, but also shared with his father a temperament that was unusual here. The first five years that Charlotte's was his and his alone, he was often to work at nine in the morning and did not leave until after midnight. On one level, his hard work paid off. The restaurant had never been more successful. Though there was little population to speak of, to eat at Charlotte's on a Monday you needed to call a week in advance. Many of the regulars, even those who considered it heresy to say it out loud, had come to the conclusion that Charlie Jr. was a better chef than his old man.

To be fair, he was a similar cook to his father. They both believed in taking the best ingredients and treating them simply. The difference was that Charles Sr. had done things the same way for so long, simple regional cooking, French and Italian country cooking, that if you were inclined to be critical you might say that the food was incredible, but that it never changed. The coq au vin of twenty years ago was the same coq au vin still on the menu. And while there is a lot to be said for keeping faith with the past, sometimes small changes lead to improvement.

So during those years when Charlie first had the restaurant, he began to introduce ideas his father would not have thought of. Things he would practice on himself on those Sundays when he did not need to leave the house on Signal Ridge. Stuff he picked up from books, from television. Using Japanese wasabi to spice a salad of wild-crafted greens. Braising poussin in soy, cloves, and star anise as they did in China. Marinating strips of lamb in Moroccan spices, cinnamon blending with the gaminess of the meat to become almost indiscernible, a low note of sweet smokiness that lifted the entire dish.

The result of all this was that Charlie did not have a life be-

yond the restaurant. By the time he was twenty-five he looked
easily ten years older. His hair was receding and his clear blue
eyes now had small bags underneath them. He did not sleep
enough. There was no time for women. All he did was work and
cook and dream of cooking and work. He noticed the world
around him less and less. Summer sunsets over Hunger Mountain. Winter snowstorms when the snow piled high against the
side of the house. The spring rain. All of it was out of focus to
him. He could only see the food on the plate. What he was creat-
ing and the precision of it as it left the kitchen. He could only see
the work, and while there was beauty in that, all beauty needs
context. Charlie's father, for all his flaws, had understood that,
and Charlie used to. In a short span of time, he no longer did.

IN MARCH of the year Charlie turned twenty-five, as the days grew
consistently warm, sometimes even touching the mid-seventies,
the winter's snowpack began to melt faster than it should. Mud
season began in earnest, the roads impassable in places, and
business at Charlotte's slowed as a result. Streambeds in the
woods that had been dry for more than a decade now ran hard
and fast with white water. The ice on Mirror Lake began its slow
melt, moving away from the shorelines, turning from a hard
white to a pigeon gray. The water ran consistently off the roof of
the restaurant and at the old farmhouse on Signal Ridge the roof
leaked steadily in the bedroom that had belonged to Charlie's
parents. Every day when he returned home he emptied out the
large bucket he had placed there and then returned it to collect
for the next day. The first sounds of spring appeared in the air,

birds in the morning that no one saw but that could be heard singing in the half dark of dawn. And on the Dog River the ice upstream began to break up and start its seasonal crawl southward.

The river flooded every year, though generally the flood took the form of water in the fields that bordered it, in new paths it carved through the forest.

Once in a man's lifetime, though, all of the elements came together in such a way that a larger flood was certain to happen. The last time it had happened in Eden was 1937. Charlie, like nearly everyone who grew up here, had seen the pictures. Men wearing suits and hats riding canoes down Main Street. Cattle swept up in the raging river water, found dead three miles from the farm where they lived. Iron trestle bridges broken away from their moorings, left in pieces at a bend in the turbulent river. Most of the buildings in the low-lying part of the town dated to that year as they replaced ones that had existed previously.

Charlie remembered that it was something his father had been concerned about because of where the restaurant was situated. Charlotte's had fire insurance but it did not have flood insurance. No company would insure it because it was built on a floodplain. Normally, in the spring, the water came onto the floodplain, as it was meant to, but it was never closer than a hundred yards away. A bad year was when the basement filled partway with water and they needed to run two or three sump pumps to clear it.

Meanwhile, March turned into April. The warm weather continued and the snow left the lowlands, though it was still deep in the woods. The Dog River overflowed its banks, and behind Charlotte's you could see where it took over the woods, instant marshland, white birch trees sticking out of the water.

And then the rain came.

It was a Tuesday. It started slowly, a light drizzle under cloudy skies, but by late afternoon as they were readying for the first diners at Charlotte's, it was falling hard. All that night the rain fell in torrents over the hills and valleys of Eden. On Wednesday it slowed for a bit but then picked up to where it had been the previous night. The soggy earth could not hold any more of it and pastures were filled with pockets of standing water. The river began to rise beyond its already swollen heights. It moved farther into the woods and from the bridges that crossed it you could look down and see the swirling white water.

From the back porch of the restaurant, Charlie watched the water, the river, the woods, and he knew it was rising, but he was not overly concerned. It rose every year and sometimes it flooded. The schoolhouse had survived the great flood. And Charlie had never seen the building threatened. Despite the heavy rain he did not expect it to be any different this time. Still, the river was moving out into the floodplain, increasing its reach with eddies of debris-strewn water circling closer toward where he stood.

Thursday brought more rain, and Friday when it was still raining, Althea called to say her road had been washed out by the brook that gave it its name and she could not get through. The radio carried news of a flash flood warning and late that afternoon Charlie took a call from the fire chief.

"Charlie," he said.

"Hi, Len." Charlie knew him from around town, though he was not a customer at the restaurant. He was a big man, with a handlebar mustache and a head of thick gray hair.

"How are things up your way?"

"It's rising pretty good but still out a good way in the fields. I think we'll be fine."

There was silence on the other end of the line, as if Len was chewing this over. "Yup," he said. "Listen, if it doesn't stop raining, we're going to need to break up the last blockage of ice upstream at Fisher's Bend or we'll have a hell of a lot of water on Main Street. What that means for your place, I don't know. But my guess is that there will be a whole lot more river there than there is now."

Charlie took this in. "What are you thinking, Len?"

"I'm worried about your business, Charlie. I would definitely close. That's a no-brainer at this point. With the way the roads are, I don't think too many folks are heading out anyway. But your building could be in danger. I hope not, but it could be. The town should be fine, once we break up the jam. You're the only one on that part of the river. What I'm offering is our help. Tomorrow morning we can send some of the boys over to do some sandbagging. Hopefully it won't be necessary. But if it is, it sure could help."

Charlie sighed, thought about this. His father would have said no way, that the Benders took care of their own place and did not need help from anyone else, no matter what the issue. But he weighed this against the possibility of losing Charlotte's, all he had ever known, a place that was in his blood.

"Thanks, Len," he said. "I hope we don't need it. But I appreciate it."

When Charlie hung up, he called Joe Collins and Peg and Althea and told all of them they were closing. That they were expecting the river to continue to grow. He told them about the fire department. About the sandbagging. He told them to take the weekend off, and though they all offered to help, he told them not to worry about it. There was nothing they could do at this point.

Charlie then called all the reservations they had and told them the score. That night he cooked for himself inside Charlotte's, and he drank a bottle of wine and sat on the porch and watched the rain fall in the black night. He could hear the river rushing through the woods. He could hear its edges sloshing on the floodplain a few hundred yards away. He watched it until the wine was gone and his eyes grew heavy.

He slept fitfully on a makeshift bed on the dining-room floor, and when he woke to a near-lightless dawn, it appeared to be raining even harder than it had the day before, spilling off the roof so quickly that to look out the windows was like trying to see through the back side of a waterfall.

CHARLIE MADE a pot of coffee, and while it brewed he went out back to the porch. The floodplain had been transformed overnight, almost half of it now underwater and you could no longer tell where the river began and where it ended. Grayish black water flowed quickly around trees. The rain fell steadily.

Inside, he walked down the narrow, rickety basement stairs. It was a typical Vermont cellar, low-ceilinged and earthen-floored. There was standing water, almost two feet of it. Charlie put on his waders and walked into it to the recess in the middle of the floor where the sump pump was. He held his breath for a moment as he reached down and turned the pump on. Playing with electricity in deep water. But he heard the machine click. Charlie found the hose and pushed it through the window and out. More water began to spill out onto the floodplain.

There was not much else he could do now, so he drank his coffee and made himself an omelet with cheddar and mushrooms and ate it with yesterday's bread. He tried to ignore the rain but it was difficult for it was everywhere, the only sound beyond the clank of his dishes when he placed them in the sink.

By ten o'clock, the first of the volunteer firefighters began to arrive. Men in pickup trucks with sirens on their dashboards who stood in huddled groups oblivious to the rain and smoked cigarettes. Charlie went and greeted them, brought them mugs of coffee. They exchanged pleasantries, talked about the rain, and like the chief, Charlie knew some of them from around town, in the roundabout way that people in small towns know one another, but none of them he ever remembered seeing inside of Charlotte's. He recognized one of them from school, Kevin O'Connor, and though it had been a long time, he looked the same, reed-thin and clean-shaven.

"Kevin," said Charlie. They shook hands.

"The chief should be here shortly," Kevin said. "And a truck with sand."

Charlie nodded. "I really appreciate you guys coming out," he said.

Kevin shrugged. "It's what we do."

More arrived and Charlie stayed busy bringing them coffee, freshening up those who already had some. The men did not seem to mind the rain. They stood and talked and smoked and they seemed happy to be away from their homes, to have the company of other men, and it occurred to Charlie that this was something he did not have in his own life. Not since Owen left.

Other than Joe Collins, who was a strong and steady presence but would go entire days without saying much more than a few words, Charlie was now used to working only with women.

Soon the chief arrived, the only full-time employee, and though the men were volunteers, Charlie could see they respected his authority. Shortly after the chief's arrival a dump truck came, and right in the parking lot of Charlotte's, where cars would normally park on a night when dinner service was going on, it dropped a large pile of sand.

The men got to work. Charlie joined them and they worked on all sides of the massive pile, filling burlap bags with sand. Some of the men formed a bucket brigade that led from the parking lot out to the floodplain. When each bag was filled and tied it was passed down the line to the last men, who began to build a levee. It was hard work and the rain was soaking through their clothes but no one appeared to mind.

By early afternoon the pile was half gone, and out on the floodplain, Charlie could see that they had the makings of a pretty good levee, bags stacked high and stretching longer than the length of the building. Charlie stopped what he was doing and went and found the chief where he was supervising the brigade.

"Think these guys would like some lunch?" Charlie asked.

"You put it out," the chief said, "I'm sure they'll eat it."

"All right," Charlie said.

In the kitchen, while the rain continued to fall, he could see the men continuing to build a high wall against the river that raged ever closer. Charlie cooked quickly and he was still soaked through but he did not care. He browned meat in a large stockpot and diced onions and garlic for the chili. To the meat he added fresh chilies, ground dried chilies, cumin, the onions and garlic, beans from a can, and the first of the season's hothouse tomatoes. It was not anything he would have served in the dining room, but it would be hot and warm and filling, and he knew that for those who were working so hard to save something that they had no personal stake in, this was all that mattered.

For an hour he let the chili cook down, the flavors all mingling together, and he returned to the building of the levee. For a while the rain slowed, which made the work easier, but as they grew closer to finishing the wall it started up again, and the river water began lapping against the base of the bags.

"Do you think it will hold?" Charlie asked the chief.

"Time will tell," Len said. "We've taken it as far as we can, I think."

Charlie set up a makeshift mess line in the dining room and the men, all of them soaking wet and tired, filed through and filled large bowls with the chili. They ate at the tables in the dining room, and since Charlie did not ask them to take their boots off— partially a show of gratitude but also not wanting to seem too uptight—water and mud pooled around their feet while they ate. The chili could have used a few more hours, but it was spicy and good and most of the firefighters returned for seconds. Charlie managed to eat some as well, though his mind was on the river, and while he knew it was out of his hands, he also knew that it was going to be a long night.

After lunch, some of the men lingered out in the parking lot and smoked but most of them got in their trucks and drove down the wet roads to their homes, to their next call. Charlie talked with the chief under the eaves of the front door. They looked at the rain and Charlie thanked him profusely for the work.

"I hope it's enough," said the chief. "You should go home, Charlie. There's nothing you can do by being here and if things really pick up you could be in trouble. It only looks like water, but if it gets rolling it can be dangerous."

Charlie nodded. "I know it."

"But you're not going anywhere, are you?" said Len.

"Probably not, Chief," Charlie said.

"I figured as much," he said. "Well, hang in there."

Charlie watched him go, stopping to admonish some of the men for their smoking, and they laughed with him and then turned back to one another, none of them appearing to be in a rush to go home, the rain falling onto their yellow coats and then to the ground. The chief climbed into his bright red pickup and gave a big wave, drove off toward Eden center. In time all the men left and Charlie thanked them as they did, and then he returned inside, to a river that was swelling beyond his kitchen, moving in eddies closer and closer to the walls of Charlotte's.

9

He was in the restaurant with nothing to do. The wan gray light of day began to disappear. The rain continued its steady and incessant fall, sometimes coming in sheets that rippled in great waves across the whole of the floodplain, other times slowing to a near drizzle before picking up again. The river water rose, the bottom bags on the levee soaked through.

After a while, Charlie went out the back door to the small porch that overlooked the floodplain and the river. The dark was thick and it was difficult to see through the falling rain. Twenty yards away he could make out the gray white sandbags that made up the levee. The sound of water was everywhere, all around him, moving loudly in the dark closer and closer to him.

There were gradations of sound, the loudest being the river water at its ambiguous center. It rushed like a train.

Charlie walked off the porch and the rain immediately soaked his hair and his clothes. He walked toward the levee, his boots making deep impressions in the soft earth. Thin light from the kitchen glowed behind him while in front it seemed to get darker and darker. There was no sky. Only rain and water and darkness.

Before he reached the levee, he stepped into pooled water up to his ankles. It was cold and wet and he thought: the levee's broken. But as he got closer he realized the levee was still there, the black river water lapping against its sides, about halfway to the top, and what he had stepped in had been only what had risen up through the earth.

Still, for the first time that day it sank in that this was for real. That if the water kept rising he might lose the restaurant, or worse. He wondered if the firefighters had broken the ice jam yet or not. He remembered the chief saying that once that happened, there could be a whole lot more river here than there was now. Charlie imagined a great wall of water moving through the trees, coming across the floodplain so fast he had no time to react before it took him with it. Picked the schoolhouse off its foundation and brought it downstream, too. He would fight like hell but the currents would be too strong, and when he finally went down, it would not hurt. It would just be quiet, and strangely comforting, like lying in a tub and slipping completely under for a second.

And as he thought this, Charlie wondered if anyone besides his mother, and Owen, wherever he was, would miss him. Truly miss him. There were the waitresses and Joe Collins and the people who made deliveries and the regulars and those, like some of the firemen, that he knew from around town. But for most of them it would be a tragedy, something to talk about, as distant as the news on television. It wouldn't mean anything. An addendum to the story they already told about his father.

Charlie couldn't do anything about the river. It would do what it needed to do and where it stopped, it stopped. But the loneliness he felt saddened him very much. It was easy to forget about when you worked as often as he did. But standing on the floodplain in the dark rain, an empty restaurant behind him, he vowed to do something about it. No matter what happened this night.

HE TRIED to keep himself busy. He mopped the dining room floor. He scrubbed the iron stove. He checked the sump pump several times. He opened a bottle of good wine and then grilled a pair of lamb chops with only salt and pepper. He washed spinach and put it in a bowl. Dressed it with lemon, olive oil, and salt. He ate standing up at the wooden table in the kitchen. The food helped him. He had only picked at the chili at lunch. He was suddenly tired and his arms hurt and he wondered from what and then he remembered the sandbagging earlier in the morning. Unfamiliar exercise. He thought about driving back to Signal Ridge, sleeping in his own bed. As the chief had said, there was nothing else he could do. But Charlie also knew that in rain like this it was not only the river you had to worry about. Streams sometimes blew up out of nowhere and wiped out roads and whatever might be on them. There were lots of little brooks between the restaurant and his house. He was better off here.

He poured himself a snifter of Armagnac and returned to the

porch. He sat down on the wooden bench and looked out into the dark and listened to the river. Suddenly he thought of his father, how much time he had spent out here smoking and looking in the same direction that Charlie did now. His father had never waited out a flood here, a real flood. Not like this. He had worried more about snow collapsing the roof, or a kitchen fire. While these were always concerns, this had to be the greatest threat Charlotte's had ever had, thought Charlie. And it was happening on his watch. The restaurant had never felt more like it belonged to him.

Charlie drank half of his drink and then he put the snifter down. He was very tired. He closed his eyes for a moment and leaned back against the wall, his feet splayed out in front of him on the porch. He fell asleep.

Hours later he woke with a start. His head had slipped on the wall and he came to in a near panic. Where was the river?

He opened his eyes. Some of the dark had lifted and the light was a muted gray. The rain had stopped. The river had receded but he could see where it still moved through the trees, white water swirling around the bone white birch. The waters had crested and Charlotte's was safe. The floodplain was full of debris and standing water. Above, the sky was turbulent and fast-moving. A stiff warm breeze blew. Wispy black clouds cut across the floodplain at eye level.

Later the sun would emerge and the drying of Eden would begin. Twin sun dogs would appear on either side of Hunger Mountain, like stained-glass windows in the sky. The river would return to where it had always been. Charlie hoped the same would not be said for the course of his life.

10

It was not until June that he called Althea and Peg and Joe Collins into the kitchen and told them what he had decided after the flood. It was midafternoon and already hot with the sun coming through the windows and he kept it short. He was not one for staff meetings.

"I'm going to look for another cook," he said, standing in front of the stove, the three of them arrayed in front of him, leaning against the big wooden table. "I have no idea how long it will take. We need the right person. Someone who knows how to execute all the dishes, can figure them out fast. But also someone who gets it, if you know what I mean. Who knows what we're trying to do."

"Can I say something?" Peg asked in her nasally voice. Peg didn't talk much. She had been around forever and Althea usually spoke for her. Charlie had come to think of them as one person.

"Yeah, of course, Peg," Charlie said. "What is it?"

"I think it's the right thing," she said. "You can't keep going the way you have been. No one could. Not even your father."

"She's right," Althea said. "You're too young, Charlie, to work this hard."

"How 'bout you, Joe?" Charlie said.

Joe nodded. "Help is always good, you know."

"That settles it, then," said Charlie.

That week he took out small ads in the newspapers across the state. The ad read: *Cook wanted to assist chef-owner at Charlotte's, a small Northeast Kingdom restaurant. Country French and Italian bistro fare. Must be flexible, creative, hardworking. Send résumé and letter stating philosophy of food to P.O. Box 119, Eden, Vermont 05843.*

After the first weekend of advertising, he got three applications, and after the second, there were fourteen more. At night at the old farmhouse, Charlie went through them one by one, reading the letters, looking at the qualifications of each. On paper, there were many strong candidates. Men and women who worked at the large ski resorts and wanted a different experience. A few from places like Boston who were relocating up north and had worked in big-city restaurants. A number of recent culinary-school graduates. These interested him the least. He did not know anyone who had gone to culinary school. His father had liked to say that those schools turned out robots. Technically sound chefs who lacked the feel one had who grew up in a culture of food. Charlie did not know if this was true but on some level it made sense to him. In truth he did not know what he wanted, only that he needed someone.

In the end, he chose the five he liked best out of the pile. He chose them because what they had to say about food mirrored his own views. Find the best ingredients you can. Learn from the land and the water around you. Sometimes the simplest way is the best way. Honor the past and specific traditions. Don't be afraid to try new things.

Charlie had each candidate come on a different morning before he began the prep. He gave them a brief tour, talked about Charlotte's, its history, the food, and then he asked them to roast a chicken while he watched. His father had often said that the measure of a restaurant is how good their roast chicken is. In other words, if you can do the easy things right, the rest should fall into place.

They were all capable chefs. The first, a pudgy middle-aged man who had cooked in Montreal, slow-roasted the bird with duck fat in a low oven. It took forever and by the time the chicken was done, Charlie had already decided he couldn't work with the man. He talked too much. And as he had only shared the kitchen with the taciturn Joe Collins all these years, it felt intrusive, regardless of how good the bird tasted.

The other four fared no better in Charlie's eyes. Two were women, two were men, and one of each was in his twenties, the others in their late thirties. They had a range of experience from busy mountain resorts to high-end suburban Boston restaurants. All of them would have done a fine job and deep down Charlie knew this. But he could not imagine hiring any of them. He had not realized how intimate a place his kitchen was. How much he had grown used to working alone. What he wanted in an assistant he could not have: his brother, or even better, another version of himself. Someone he could work with in silence who knew as well as he did what they were trying to do and how to do it.

Charlie told all five of them he was going to sleep on it and would get back to them. He thanked them for coming in and their interest in Charlotte's. The following week he called each of them back and apologized and said that he was going in a different direction. He threw out the rest of the applications. His need for help was real. But it was going to be harder to let a stranger into his kitchen than he had thought.

ONE MORNING a few weeks later Charlie was at the wooden table filleting a wild salmon when he heard what sounded like someone trying to open the door off the back porch. Charlie put his knife down and wiped his hands on a towel and opened the wooden door. The screen door was latched and through it he saw a dark-haired woman wearing a baseball hat.

"Oh," she said, "Charlie. The front door was locked."

Charlie unlatched the door. She looked familiar but he couldn't place her. "How are you?" she said.

"I'm fine," said Charlie, and she took off her hat and her hair fell out from under it and he recognized her. It was Claire Apple.

"Claire," he said. "Jesus, I didn't know it was you."

"It's been a while," she said.

"Well, come on in," said Charlie, and he stepped aside.

Claire walked past him. She wore jeans and a loose-fitting T-shirt, sandals on her feet. She stopped in front of the wooden table and she looked around the room. "I never got to come back in the kitchen," she said. "But this is what I imagined it looked like."

She turned around and faced Charlie. She smiled.

"You're back in Eden?" he said.

"Yes. For a couple of months now."

Charlie nodded. He was puzzled and felt suddenly shy, incapable of maintaining eye contact with this woman in front of him whom he had known briefly many years before. He couldn't think of any reason why she might be here right now. "That's great," said Charlie.

"Yeah," she said. "It's surprising but it is."

"And everything is good?"

"Sure," she said. "It is. But I understand you're looking for help."

"Oh," said Charlie, suddenly understanding. She needed a job. "Well, not really. Though we can always use subs out front. Peg and Althea are still here. And we get some college girls who fill in on the really busy nights."

"I meant cooking," said Claire.

Charlie laughed nervously. "Cooking?"

"Yes, I'm a chef."

"I didn't know."

"How would you?" said Claire. "I haven't seen you since high school."

"And you went to Chicago, right?"

"Good memory," she said. She had her hands in her back pockets and she swayed slightly as she spoke. If anything she had grown more beautiful with age, the subtle crow's-feet coming off the corners of her eyes only drawing attention to them.

"Northwestern," she said. "Only I spent my junior year in France and fell in love with the food. When I graduated I went back and got an apprenticeship at a small family place in a small village in the south. You would have liked it a lot, I think. It was a lot like this. A little town called Agda. A storefront place. A few tables out front. The mother did most of the cooking though the daughter helped out. And then me. Nothing too fancy. You ate whatever they were cooking that day. I learned a lot."

Charlie nodded. "Sounds great."

"It was. It's a long story, but I'm back and I'd like a job. I think I could help."

Charlie shrugged. "Well, okay," he said. "I'm asking everyone to roast a chicken. Do you want to come back or—"

"Right now would be fine," said Claire, putting her hair up again, under the baseball cap, walking to the sink and washing her hands. "Tell me where to go."

Charlie set her up on the other side of the table from him. From the walk-in he brought her a chicken, a free-range a farmer had raised for him down in Rochester.

"Feel free to use the pantry, anything you need. There are fresh herbs on the windowsill there. Anything else, just ask."

"Sure," said Claire, and she smiled at him. Charlie sat down on a stool so he would not appear to be hovering over her. Claire took the bird and in the sink she washed it inside and out and then dried it. She laid it on the table. Next she chopped onions and lemons into a small dice and from the plant growing on the windowsill she took several sprigs of rosemary. Some of these she left intact while with the others she separated the needles from the branches and rough-chopped them and added them to the small bowl in which she had placed the onions and lemons. She anointed this mixture with olive oil and stuffed the cavity of the bird with it.

She rubbed the whole chicken with olive oil, seasoned it with salt and pepper, and Charlie admired the way she used the salt, the most important thing in the kitchen, the way she measured it without thinking with her thumb and index finger.

"Is your grill on?" Claire asked.

"Yes," Charlie said, and she went to it then, laid the bird on the grate, skillfully turning it several times to give it the grill marks and the smoky flavor, and then removed it to one of the old frying pans, bent and black with age.

She turned the oven to 425 and then began to work on her side dishes.

From the pantry she grabbed a large red potato and Charlie watched as she cut this into half-inch dice. She cubed a carrot and she tossed both the carrot and the potato around the chicken.

"Stock?" she asked.

"In the cooler," said Charlie. "Those plastic jugs when you walk in."

In a moment she was back, and she poured a little of the good dark chicken stock around the bird, and added a little brandy from the bottle above the stove as well, and then when the oven had reached temperature, she placed the pan inside on the middle rack.

"What do you have for vegetables? Haricots verts?"

"There's some green beans in the fridge."

Claire went to the small fridge against the far wall and from it she took a handful of the green beans, frenched them, and then quickly blanched them in boiling salty water, letting them cool in an ice bath, bringing out their color.

"How long will your chicken roast?" Charlie asked.

"Twenty-three minutes."

"That's rather exact, don't you think?"

"I could be wrong," said Claire. "But I gave it a good grilling and it's a small bird and a hot oven."

"Okay," said Charlie, "we have some time, then. Do you have questions about the job?"

"I do," said Claire, coming toward him. She veered away and took the other stool that was against the wall and brought it over next to Charlie. She pulled the stool within a foot of him and sat down and she looked at him with her dark eyes and once again he had to look away.

"What are you looking for?" Claire said.

Charlie thought about this. The truth was that he was looking for her. There was no question. He had been around her for all of thirty minutes, and all of a sudden he was aware of his heart, of the blood running like a stream through his veins, of its steady pumping. He was aware of his hands folded on his lap. She made him uneasy and comfortable at the same time. But mostly she made him feel present in a way that made him realize that he had not been for a long time; that despite how hard he worked he had been going through the motions, serious and dedicated, yes, but also somehow absent.

Charlie forced himself to look her in the eye. "I'm looking for someone who can hold their own in this kitchen. It gets busy. And we don't have the support that other restaurants have— prep cooks and pastry chefs and the whole nine yards. It's just us. So I need someone reliable and hardworking. Creative. Someone who," Charlie said, and he laughed as he said it, "can be another version of me."

Claire smiled. "I'm your gal," she said, and she laughed.

"You think so?" Charlie said, admiring her confidence.

"Yup," said Claire.

"I haven't tasted the chicken yet," said Charlie.

HOLDING A towel in her hand, Claire reached into the oven and removed the hot pan. She took the bird out of it and put it on a cutting board to rest. She removed the cubed potatoes and the julienned carrots. She dumped most of the liquid out of the pan and then added back some of the stock and a glass or so of white wine, and Charlie watched as it came to a rapid boil.

While the sauce was reducing, Claire returned the bright green haricots verts to a frying pan and added a good pat of butter and some lemon juice and she shook the pan and then seasoned the beans with salt and pepper.

Next she carved the chicken. Her knife work was expert, and she frenched the thighbone where it came off the breast and plated the pieces of meat in the center, using the roasted root vegetables as a bed, removing several thin slices of the breast on the bias and laying these against the thigh. She strained the sauce through a chinois and while it was filtering through the fine mesh she placed a handful of the bright green beans on one side of the chicken. She spooned the sauce on the meat and in a circle moving away from it on the side of the plate opposite the beans. She quick-chopped some parsley sprigs and these with a quick flick of her wrists she tossed over everything. She pushed the plate across toward Charlie.

"Voilà!" she said.

Charlie looked at it, and shook his head as if in mock disapproval. "I'm not sure it's up to the standards of Charlotte's," he said.

"Oh, be quiet and just taste it," said Claire.

And he did, he tasted it, and it was just what it should be, moist and satisfying, the flavor of the lemon and the rosemary at once bright and earthy. The green beans were crisp and perfect. All of it seasoned with a light touch even his father would have appreciated.

"You can really cook," he said.

"Don't act so surprised," said Claire.

"When can you start?"

"Are you serious?" she said, a wide smile lighting up her face, her eyes.

"You bet," said Charlie.

That night, back at the farmhouse after service, Charlie grilled himself a venison steak, which he ate on the porch with a salad of early tomatoes and goat cheese. After, he sat and watched the full moon over the mountains and slowly worked through a bottle of Burgundy. In his mind, he replayed the day over and over again, Claire at the back door, her story about France. Her skillful cooking. It all seemed somewhat unreal to him.

He noticed that she had not been wearing a ring. Not that she would ever think of him that way. A long time ago she had been Owen's girl and now she would be Charlie's employee. She needed a job and seemed to know what she was doing. The chicken was excellent. And what she didn't know he could teach her. But that was in the future. She didn't start for another week and when she did he would have to be professional. Until then, he could indulge himself a little. He closed his eyes and he saw her as she had appeared that afternoon. Her dark eyes, the pale lovely skin, the outline of her breasts beneath her loose T-shirt. Her hair as it fell to her shoulders when she removed her hat.

11

Claire Apple thought she had left Eden behind for good. When she was eighteen the only thing she loved about Eden was Owen, but then his father killed himself and like that he moved out into the world and she never heard from him again. She, too, wanted out, from as early as she could remember. She dreamed of big cities and of a life different from her parents'. She found the narrow dirt roads and the steep hills confining. She wanted to taste all that she had read about in books and seen in films. She did not want to be one of those girls she grew up with who wanted to dream but did not know how. Who sought husbands as soon as they were able and built houses on lots next to their parents and settled into the only life they would ever know by the time they were twenty. A couple of kids and a summer of looking forward to deer season when the men went to camp and she had a few weeks when she could pretend to be on her own.

Though sometimes during those first years of college she got homesick and she remembered the quiet ease of living in a place where you knew everyone and they knew you. Where you were the prettiest girl and the best student. Unlike college, where Claire thought that there were lots of girls prettier, and plenty of people smarter. She had boyfriends but none of them seemed to last very long. She went through a time when she closed herself off to men. She could not give herself up as she had with Owen. They had only been kids but she had never felt so loved. On summer nights when they had snuck out of their respective houses, they would share a sleeping bag at the lake, and though they were already sleeping together, on many of these nights they would just lie in a locked embrace, not moving, not speaking, feeling the warmth of each other's skin, falling asleep with their faces touching. He said "I love you" first and when he did she cried. They said it all the time then. It made them feel adult and she trusted him more than she had ever trusted anyone.

Sometimes in Chicago, Claire returned to that time in her mind and she wondered if Owen would still try to find her. He had not called like he said he would but part of her held out hope. She knew her parents would not willingly give him her address—they were glad when it broke off, regardless of how it happened—but she kept imagining him trying to find her, showing up at her dorm one night, as if only a week, and not two years, had passed.

But as time went on she thought about this less and less until she did not think about it anymore.

For her junior year, she had the opportunity to go abroad and Claire chose Paris. A lot of friends were heading to Asia, and Paris had become a cliché for many of the students, but Claire didn't care. She had an art history minor to go with her English major. She knew a little French. She had read Hemingway and Stein and she wanted to experience the cafés and the museums and the food. She wanted the blatant romance of it all and she was unapologetic about it.

She fell in love with the city right away. She could be anything she wanted there. Sometimes walking down those wide avenues, she liked to imagine that she was a native, that she knew these streets better than anyone. She'd pass Americans looking over a map on the corner and she'd move right past them, as if she couldn't understand a word they had to say.

As part of her program, she took classes at the Sorbonne. It was there that she met Étienne.

He was forty-two years old, exactly twice her age, and taught survey classes on the masters. He spoke English well and was Claire's idea of a Frenchman. One of the French girls in her class warned her against him. That he had a different girl every year, many of them Americans. But Claire did not care. He was slender, his black hair graying at the temples. He wore nice suits with vests and smoked Gauloises. He could not be more different from the boys she had known. And though she knew it was horribly predictable for her to sleep with him, part of her wanted to do it for precisely this reason. She laughed about it with one of her friends on the phone. He was just another part of Paris, like the Louvre or the Eiffel Tower. Something you had to visit before you went home.

Though in short time, it became more than that. Claire essentially moved into his sunny second-floor apartment. She spent all her time there. In the mornings they made love in the light of day and she loved being naked in front of him. She loved having his hands on her, and after, he would get them both breakfast and they would lie in bed. She'd watch him smoke and they talked in French. One afternoon he came home with a dress for her, red and clingy, and it was never anything she would have bought for herself and when she put it on he nodded approvingly. That night they ate big bowls of mussels at a sidewalk café, and when they walked home afterward, they held hands and Claire was aware of how men stared at her, at her body beneath the silk, and it surprised her how much she liked the attention.

Claire didn't want the year to end. In May she was due to fly back to the States and as it grew closer she became sadder and sadder about it. One night she told Étienne this and he shrugged and said, "Don't go."

"What am I going to do?"

"Come south with me for the summer. To the coast."

Claire laughed. "Yeah," she said. "That's realistic."

"You can work at my mother's restaurant," he said. "Pay your way. And then in the fall you can come back here if you want."

"That sounds nice," said Claire.

She began to think about it, though, and the more she thought about it the more it seemed possible. A week before she was to return home she called her mother and told her she was staying, that Étienne had offered her a job in his family's restaurant for the summer. When her mother asked who Étienne was she did not lie to her.

"Oh, Claire, please," her mother said. "Your professor? You have to be joking."

And when the summer came to an end and it was time for her to return to Paris, Françoise asked her if she would stay. Étienne said she should. Claire was honored they would want her and she said yes. Françoise treated her like a daughter, Marthe like a sister, and on weekends she had Étienne in her apartment. She had the food and spoke French better with each passing day and was happy. If she had any doubts at all, they were about Étienne, who had brought her into this life.

He seemed content with how things were. He said he loved how easily she fit into his family. How good she had become in the kitchen. And he still looked her in the eye as he had when they first met, and he still liked to stay in bed late on weekend mornings and make love with the sun coming through the windows. But he never talked about the future, about marriage, or her returning to Paris, and sometimes Claire wondered how long they could continue like this.

But mostly she did not dwell on it, and as one year in France turned into two and then three, she moved completely into the village life and it was her own.

One Friday afternoon she boarded the train to Paris to see Étienne. It was a warm sunny day and from the train she saw the first flowers of the season at the edge of the farm fields. She hoped they could have one of those nights that they used to have, when they first met, drinking wine and eating at one of his favorite cafés. Having espressos somewhere else. Coming home and moving together in front of the large open windows in the dark.

When she reached his building, she bounded up the old staircase and when she got to his door it was slightly ajar. He was home. Claire opened the door slowly.

She stood with her back to Claire, her head down as she

combed long strands of blond hair. She was tall and slender and she wore no clothes.

"Étienne," the girl said with an American accent, and then she turned around and saw Claire in the doorway. "Who are you?" she asked.

Claire stared at her. She was pretty with small breasts. She was probably eighteen, but she looked even younger. Claire shook her head.

"I should be asking you that," she said.

Claire turned and left. She should have known better, she thought. On the street Étienne came toward her, with a bag of groceries in his arms, and when he saw her he looked surprised. Claire crossed the street and he called to her but she began to run. He didn't catch her until the train station.

"Claire," he said. "What are you doing?"

"I saw the girl."

"So?"

She wanted to hit him. "So? That's what you have to say?"

"I never promised you anything."

"You knew I was coming today."

"I thought later, I don't know."

"I'm going home," she said, and she turned her back on him. Étienne did not go after her this time.

Back in the village she didn't have to say anything to Françoise and Marthe. They knew. Claire packed her things, and when she said good-bye to the two women in the restaurant's kitchen, she cried though they just hugged her, kissed her on each cheek. Claire wondered if they had been through this exact thing before. Françoise said Étienne was on his way down from Paris, that he wanted to see her before she left.

"I'm not going to wait," Claire said.

Françoise nodded. She knew her son.

The next day, Claire flew into Boston. She took a bus to Montpelier and then called a cab for the ride to Eden. She had forgotten how lovely the hills were in the spring. The first green on the trees.

Her mother answered the door and broke down first. It had been almost four years. "Oh, Claire," she said as she hugged her.

Claire couldn't stop crying. She saw her father standing behind them.

"I'm sorry," Claire sobbed.

"We're just glad you're home," her father said.

Together they moved inside.

12

When she first returned home, Claire barely left her bed for a week. She slept the day away and emerged in her nightgown for coffee and breakfast in the late afternoon. She blamed it on jet lag but both she and her parents knew better. She was depressed. She had no idea what she was going to do. She had no money and did not want a loan from her parents. She knew her parents expected her to return to school but she had no interest in doing so. She had finished three years and then in France she learned all she wanted to know: what it was she was good at, what she wanted to do with her life.

She wanted to cook, she knew that. The question was where and this was too overwhelming for her to think about. She needed to get to New York or back to Chicago or someplace where she could talk her way into a kitchen. She had no idea how to make this happen. Instead all she did was sleep and mope around in her old bedroom. She thought about Étienne and about France and sometimes she cried. She knew she was right to have left but it hurt anyway.

One evening she wandered into the kitchen and both her parents were at the table. They looked up when she came in. Her father said, "Here's a crazy idea."

"What?" said Claire, slightly exasperated, expecting another bid for her to finish her degree.

"Charlotte's is looking for a chef."

Claire leaned against the counter. "Charlotte's," she repeated, as if hearing the name for the first time.

"You remember, the Benders' restaurant?"

"Of course, it's just been a long time since I thought about that. It's still open?"

"Oh yes," her mother said. "It's doing really well. The son—Charlie—runs it. We go now and again and the food is always excellent."

Claire thought about this. "I'm trying to move on. Not that I don't want to be near you, just not this near. You know? Charlotte's is a little close to home."

"We know," her father said. "Think about it this way. Do it for six months. Save some money. Have another notch on your résumé. They do a nice job there. If you're serious about this cooking thing, it'll only make you better."

For the first time in many years, Claire found herself thinking about Owen Bender. The funny thing was that she knew nothing about food back then, never really thought about it beyond when she was hungry and wanted to eat. She didn't remember him talking about the restaurant much, except that he was always there working when they were not together. She had eaten there, of course, a long time ago, and she knew it was very pretty. Small. Not dissimilar from what she knew in France. If Owen were still there she could not work there. That would be too strange. But Charlie, his quiet brother, was always kind to her. She thought they would get along fine.

CHARLOTTE'S DELIGHTED Claire. After her interview, he had shown her the rest of the restaurant and she had forgotten how lovely that front room was, with its wide-board floors and tangerine walls. The kitchen reminded her of France, more of a farmhouse kitchen than a commercial one. Windows that looked out to the river. Plenty of light.

And she felt completely at ease. Not even the slightest of flutters in her stomach. From the moment Charlie greeted her at the door, and she saw him again, the pale blue eyes she had never really noticed, his face craggy for a man of his age, and shook his strong hand, she knew this was where she was meant to be. And at the worktable all distractions receded, and she was only half aware of his watching her and she did not mind it, for all she could see was the task in front of her, the roasting of the bird, the making of the sauce, the dicing of vegetables. It was as if she had never cooked anywhere else. Later, when she drove away from the restaurant, through bright summer sunshine, she could not help but smile, a wide smile that turned into a laugh, her hands leaving the steering wheel with excitement, returning again as she crossed onto the covered bridge, the Dog River beneath her.

———

IN THE week before she started work, Claire rented an apartment above the hardware store on Main Street. It was important to feel that she was on her own again, even if she was in Eden. It was not much, one bedroom, and the living room had shag carpeting. But it had a small porch on the back that looked out to the Dog River, wider and more open here than it was downstream at the restaurant. The apartment was cheap and available and convenient for work. She told herself it was just a place to sleep.

David Rubin, an old family friend with a pickup truck, helped her move some of the furniture her parents were willing to part with. After he left, she spent the time turning the small apartment into her own, moving the furniture around until she was satisfied with it, arranging what art she had on the walls, hanging a few pots and pans from the rack above the two-burner propane stove. She bought flowers from the florist in town and placed these in vases around the rooms. She laid out her jewelry, her earrings and necklaces and bracelets, on the top of her bureau. She hung her clothes in the closet. And when she was tired of working on the apartment, she poured herself a glass of wine and sat on the back porch and watched the river. She cooked simple dinners for herself. She had a space of her own, and there are times in a woman's life when that is enough.

13

There was an Indian summer that fall. It stayed warm until late October. Inside the kitchen of Charlotte's, they kept the windows open until the sun went down.

That was the fall that Charlie and Claire learned how to move around each other. In the mornings they made stocks and reductions; they marinated meat and fish; and they prepped vegetables for that evening's service. Charlie taught Claire the workings of Charlotte's, all the things that his father had taught him. How they prepared certain dishes, where everything was stored, how the inventory worked. What days the producers and growers made deliveries, who to call when they needed more meat or vegetables or other supplies.

They worked well together. Kitchens are intimate places, and even though Charlotte's was unusual in its space, oftentimes Charlie would feel Claire's thighs against the back of his legs as she moved to turn something on the grill; sometimes he would reach from behind her to shake a saucepan, and when he did so, he could smell the soap on her neck, the fragrance of the shampoo she had used that morning.

The simple fact was that with each passing day, Charlie Bender was growing more smitten with Claire Apple. He loved working with her; he loved being with her; and it was not just her physical beauty. No, that was a large part of it, certainly. But there was more. The inexpressible part of desire, an ache that comes from somewhere deep within, the part you cannot control or give voice to. Where you stay up at night not wanting to sleep for she is in your thoughts and you are afraid that the sleep will take her away, only to discover that she is still with you when you wake. It was like nothing he had ever experienced before and it scared him. It made him nervous. Like his father before him, he had grown used to being his own man, to governing his life by some internal compass that could not be adulterated by others.

There was also the fact that Charlie was Claire's boss. And there was her history with Owen, though they never talked about that, other than briefly, when he told her where Owen was, that he had not seen him since right after their father died. Charlie had no sense that Claire was even aware of his feelings, let alone that she might return them. And so, at the minimum, he needed to treat her as he would any of the people who worked for him. As it turned out, he was incapable of doing so.

As time passed those first months she was at the restaurant, he grew afraid that he wore his affection openly on his face; that both Claire and the other workers saw it in his goofy smile when he joked with her; saw it in his body language.

And so, in response, Charlie began to relate to her differently than he did to the others, than he did to Joe Collins or Althea or Peg. And he related to her not in the way he wanted to, not in the way he did when he dreamed about it; in his dreams when they were lovers.

Instead, he treated her harshly.

He criticized her work; went out of his way to taste her sauces before they made it to the plate, suggesting they were missing something when he knew they were just what they should be. Once he even snapped at her when, in the heat of service, a pot containing pasta boiled over on her watch—the most natural and innocent of mistakes—and as the water cascaded down the sides and onto the large flame he told her to pay attention. And he saw her brace when he did so, and he wished he had not said it, wished he could tell her how he really felt; wished he could explain that everything he did now was an outgrowth of the fact that he was crazy for her.

All men smitten live with a certain duality of self. Charlie Bender was no different. His only hope was that he was not building a wall between them, something from which they could not recover to reach the place where he thought they belonged.

ONE AFTERNOON in mid-October, on a day when the temperature soared into the seventies with a bright sun, Charlie was in the walk-in, kneeling on the floor, sorting through a box of fingerling potatoes, when he heard Claire behind him.

"Where are you taking me?" Claire asked.

"You'll see," he said.

"You're so cryptic, Charlie Bender," she said.

Charlie turned and looked at her. "This way," he said.

The deer run was narrow but the dirt was hardened and the hiking was not hard. The canopy was high here and in places shards of sunlight shot through to where they were and they could feel it warm on their arms. As they climbed, the hemlocks and spruce at the bottom of the hill gave way to poplars and young birches, their bark the color of sandstone, their leaves the palest of greens, almost yellow. The sun splashed through now, and its dappled light spread across the forest floor in waves. At one point they startled a whitetail and Claire said, "Look," and Charlie turned in time to see it bounding up over a small hillock and out of view.

It had been three days since Claire confronted him in the pantry and Charlie was doing his best now to treat her as an equal, without revealing the truth of his love to her. He was bringing her into everything he did.

Now, moving up the steep hillside on the deer run, Claire looked back and saw the distance they had traveled and she saw through the trees to other hills and when she looked down she could see Charlotte's as she had never seen it, from above, a little box, the sunlight catching a glint of river behind it.

"So are we going to walk all the way to Canada?" she asked.

"Work with me," said Charlie. "It's not much farther."

Soon the deer run began to level out, and Claire realized that they had crested the hill, and to her surprise it did not immediately head downhill again, but instead flattened out. Up ahead she saw bright sun and in a moment they reached a clearing

large enough for thirty people to stand in. To the west it dropped
steeply off and they could see over the trees to all of Eden. All
around them was the bright forest, and when Charlie stopped,
Claire stopped, too, and he reached out with his hand in front of
her as if to prevent her from walking another step.

"Look," he said, pointing across the clearing. "Do you see
them?"

Claire stared ahead to the far tree line and she did not know
what she was looking for. She saw the remainder of the clearing
and then the shadows of the trees, the play of the light across the
deep green leaves.

She said, "What? What should I be seeing?"

"Focus," Charlie said. "Look again."

She did. Still nothing.

"There," said Charlie, taking her hand in his own, using it to
point. "On the ground, near the trees, do you see them now?"

Suddenly Claire saw them, amazed she had not before, for
they were everywhere. She smiled. "Wow," she said, "there are
tons of them."

"This is the time," Charlie said. "My father always said it was
right after the full moon in October. They grow in great veins,
like copper or something. The window is about a week long, and
if you don't get up here, they're gone."

They moved across the clearing then, and when they got near
the woods, Charlie bent down and with his pocketknife he cut
one of the mushrooms from the earth, held it up to Claire, and
they were perfect chanterelles, yellowish brown stems, large
floppy caps. From the pocket of his jeans he removed a folded-
up trash bag and opened it. He gave Claire his other knife. They
got down on their knees onto the moist forest floor, and while a

soft warm breeze blew through the clearing they picked mushroom after mushroom, working in silence, and the only sound
that Claire could hear was the wind through the treetops, the
rustling of the bag as they filled it, the gentle click of the knife as
each chanterelle left the earth for their hands.

14

A long fall often means a harsh winter. That was the case Claire's first year at Charlotte's. The first snow came in early December and it never seemed to stop. Some days the sky was filled with big lazy flakes that never seemed to reach the ground. Other days it fell like rain, the snow piling up against the sides of the restaurant. Once a week Charlie climbed onto the roof of Charlotte's and shoveled as much as he could off. It was futile but critical work. There was always the possibility of a cave-in.

The roads were snow-covered and slick, and the only saving grace was that the banks were so high there was no danger of a car going off. Tree branches in the forest strained and groaned from the oppressive weight, some of them eventually giving way, crashing silently to the soft snow below.

In January, the mercury dipped under zero and stayed there for almost two weeks, going as low as thirty below in the deep of morning.

Then there was a brief thaw, three days of heavy snowmelt and sloppy muddy roads, before the biggest snowstorm of the year hit.

It was a classic nor'easter. What started as rain off the Carolinas became heavy snow through Pennsylvania, and when it reached New England, it met up with a smaller clipper storm coming out of Alberta. The resulting storm stalled over Vermont, Maine, and New Hampshire, unable to kick out to sea, and for twenty-four hours it snowed at a rate of several inches an hour.

From inside Charlotte's, Charlie watched it fall out the big windows. It was heavy, wet snow. This was one of those storms where no one but the plows went out. Everyone stocked up on groceries and candles and fed the woodstoves and spent time with family. Children secretly hoped the power would go out. Parents and children played board games. Time stopped.

Charlie called Peg and Althea and Joe and told them not to come in. He called Claire last, despite the fact that she arrived first, but this is what he did. By the time he called her, he got her machine. A few minutes later she walked in the door, took off her wool hat, and shook the snow from her hair.

"I must have just missed you," said Charlie. "We're not going to open."

"I figured. It's already nasty out there."

"Why'd you come in?"

"There's some things I could catch up on," Claire said,

which was true, and the idea of sitting home all day in her small apartment had little appeal. Being stuck out at her parents had even less.

Charlie nodded. "Well, you really didn't have to come in."

"Have you noticed how low we are on demi? There's only that one tray left in the freezer."

Charlie smiled. "You're worse than I am."

Claire winked at him. "Someone has to keep track around here."

In the kitchen they filled cookie sheets with marrow bones and roasted them. They chopped onions, carrots, and celery and then slow-carmelized them with butter. They filled the largest pot they had with the roasted bones, added the vegetables, whole heads of garlic, peppercorns, cloves, sprigs of thyme, bay leaf, two bottles of red wine, and then covered it all with water. They brought it to a simmer and left it.

Next they made a dark chicken stock, a light chicken stock, and a fish stock. Soon all the burners were filled with pots full of bones and vegetables and water and the air in the kitchen was rich with the smell of the different stocks. It was midafternoon. Through the windows they could see the sky dumping snow. There was nothing else they could do but wait now. Wait and watch the snow fall.

WHILE THERE was still light, Charlie got a jump on the shoveling. A plow would come and take care of the parking lot but he, or Joe Collins, usually did the walkways. The snow was heavy, and as soon as he moved it, more took its place. It was falling that fast.

He had finished the steps and was partway down the walk that led to the driveway when the door opened behind him. Claire stepped out with her hat and coat and gloves on. She grabbed the other shovel next to the door.

"You don't have to," Charlie said.

"I know," she said. "I want to."

Charlie smiled and went back to work. A moment later, he felt it.

Claire had taken a shovelful of snow and dropped it on the back of his neck. He felt the cold going down the back of his shirt.

"You didn't," Charlie said, turning around. Claire had backed off and was near the door. She laughed. "Oh, I did," she said, and she reached down with her shovel and scooped more snow and tossed it across at him. It hit the front of his down jacket with a thud.

"You're really asking for it," said Charlie.

"How about now?" asked Claire. She took another shovelful and this time it went right for his face. Charlie managed to duck some of it but the rest caught him on the cheeks and on his hat.

"That's it," he said, and he took off after her. Claire dropped her shovel and began to run toward the side of the building. The snow was deep and she screamed playfully as she ran and Charlie trudged through it after her.

"Whitewash," he called.

"You have to catch me," she said, disappearing around the side of the building.

Charlie had an advantage with his long legs but she had the head start, and when he finally gained on her she was halfway across the floodplain, and the snow was almost waist-high. He dove for her and managed to grab her shoulders as he went down, pulling her sideways onto him and into the snow. He felt her struggle to stand and he got to his feet first and with his hands he covered her with snow.

"You're so dead," she said.

Charlie kept burying her with more snow. "That's what you get," Charlie said.

Claire managed to stand and in front of him her cheeks were bright red and she shook her head and pushed him hard in the chest and he lost his balance and fell down again in the deep snow. She laughed. Charlie laughed, too. He tried to get up and fell again.

"Oh, shit," he said, and it was cold and there was snow all inside his coat but he couldn't have cared less.

"Help me up," he said, holding out his arm.

Claire took it and he pulled her down into the snow. She flipped snow at his face.

"Truce," he called.

"Truce? Are you kidding?"

"No, no. I'm serious."

Claire looked at him skeptically. "I'm not sure I trust you."

Charlie raised one arm weakly into the air. "I promise."

"All right," said Claire. They shook on it.

INSIDE THE dining room they warmed themselves in front of the woodstove. Outside the light was fading fast.

"I'm soaked," Claire said.

"Whose fault is that?"

"All right, I might have started it."

Charlie laughed. "I'll leave it at that. Listen: the roads are not going to be pretty. I can strain the stock. You should think about getting going. The wind is going to pick up. It could be whiteout soon."

Claire rubbed her hands over the stove. "Or we could have dinner."

"Have dinner?"

"Yeah. Like people do. Like people do in this room every night."

Charlie nodded. He could think of nothing he'd rather have happen. "Okay, but I'm cooking," he said.

"Sure," said Claire.

"And that means you can't come into the kitchen until I say."

"Surprise meal, then?"

"Something like that."

Claire looked at Charlie. She ran her hand through her wet hair. "Fine," she said. "But you can't come in here either, then. Until you're done. This will be my room, that can be yours."

CLAIRE SAT down on a chair in the dining room in front of the woodstove. She pulled another chair up and on this she put her feet. The fire was drawing well and she watched the orange flames in the firebox and the heat it gave off was warm. With no other noise in the dining room besides the crackling of the fire, she could hear Charlie moving around in the kitchen, pans clanking, the familiar creak of the heavy walk-in door.

Before he left, Charlie had opened a bottle of wine, a big red, an Amarone, and poured her a glass and then took the bottle with him.

Claire watched the fire and sipped her wine and asked herself what she was doing. There was something between them, she knew, and when there was something between people there were only two ways it could go. One was for both to walk away, or at least for one to walk away fast enough that the other had no choice but to give in. The other was to move inexorably toward each other so that there was no turning back. Claire thought that by being here she was choosing the latter and she did not want to think about it too hard, for she knew that if she did, the practical side of her would take over and know that there was no good that could come of it. He was her boss; she worked for him; she needed the work, and nothing tended to screw things up as much as when coworkers slept together.

On the other hand, she found herself favoring the impractical side of herself, the side of herself that was drawn to Charlie. There were plenty of men who were better-looking, she thought. He certainly did not have his brother's good looks. But he had those clear blue eyes, and he was tall and strong, and when he was not obsessive about the work in the kitchen, he showed her that he had a good heart, that he could be sensitive, and she respected his talent immensely. Every day, it seemed, she learned something new from him. Of course, that did not mean she needed to sleep with him. Have dinner, Claire, she said to herself, keep him company, but don't drink too much, and don't go to bed with him.

Claire slowly sipped her wine, felt the stove warming her feet. She looked over to the kitchen. She could hear the sounds of cooking and she smiled. Her clothes were still damp but since

commercial mixer and the long threads became a dark green linguini that would turn red when he cooked it.

On the stove he boiled water and on another burner he placed
a large sauté pan. In the pan he put a pat of butter and when the
butter began to foam he added chopped shallots and cooked
these until they were translucent. Then he added the pieces of
tail and claw and knuckle, shaking the pan while he watched the
lobster start to change color. He poured some Scotch whiskey
into the pan and then flambéed it, tilting the large pan so that the
butane flame reached up and touched it and the alcohol caught
on fire. He lifted it off the burner and shook it until the flames
extinguished. He let the whiskey sauce continue to reduce and
the lobster to cook and then he added some heavy cream. He
chopped fresh tarragon and threw a healthy handful around the
lobster. He turned the flame to low.

When the water came to a boil he tossed the fresh pasta in and
he timed its finish by going to the fridge and pulling out a bottle
of champagne, popping the cork. As soon as he did that, Charlie
strained the fresh pasta, adding a quarter cup of the starchy water
to the saucepan, loosening the sauce where it had thickened. It
was suddenly smooth and velvety and this was how he wanted it.

While he had a moment now, Charlie went to the door and
looked in on Claire. She was next to the stove, and at the moment
he looked through she was putting her jeans back on, jumping
slightly as she pulled them up over her hips. She wore only a
black bra and he got a good look at the shape of her breasts, and
a touch of thigh before her jeans came over them. She had no
idea he was seeing her, and he understood that she was drying
her clothes next to the fire, and it was a completely rational thing
for anyone to do given the circumstances, but it was sexy to him

nonetheless, the sight of her pale skin, the curve of her breasts, the red of her mouth as it opened slightly from the exertion, from the heat.

CHARLIE TOSSED the now-red pasta with butter, salt, and pepper and divided it between two stark white oval plates. He took the tail meat out of the shells but he left the claws whole and these he put on top of the pasta, scattering the tail meat around it, on the edge of the plate. He finished the dish with the sweet sauce of reduced Scotch and tarragon and cream, pouring it over everything. He quickly checked the window to make sure Claire was dressed. She was back in her clothes and she sat facing the stove.

He moved through the swinging doors like a waiter, one plate in his right hand, the other balanced higher up on his arm, his left hand holding the champagne.

"Wow," Claire said when Charlie placed one plate in front of her. He put his down on the table, and then the champagne, and then went to the bar and got two flutes.

Claire rose and moved candles from other tables and lit them and they ate in the firelight and the candlelight and there was the ticking of the stove and now and again a gust of wind against the old building. They talked about the food, about the pasta, how the roe changed the linguini from green to red, just as the lobster itself did. Claire was surprised that the Scotch worked; she thought it would be too much, too heavy, too sweet. But it lent a smokiness to the dish, a touch of sweetness and nuttiness that brought out the richness of the seafood.

Charlie explained to her how he had come up with the recipe, during one of his father's blind baskets, how his father thought he should have used brandy instead of Scotch but was surprised, as well, that it stood up the way it did. "Lobster Charles, he called it," said Charlie.

"I wish I'd known your father better," said Claire.

Charlie played with the stem of his champagne flute. "He was a complex man."

"Aren't they all?"

"More than most. He was brilliant. Bullheaded. Difficult."

"Sounds like someone else I know."

"My father and I are very different."

"How?"

"I don't know," said Charlie. "I don't like to talk about it."

"I didn't mean to pry."

Charlie looked across at her. "It's okay. I just mean that after he died everything kind of got fucked up."

"You mean between you and Owen?"

"Yeah. You were there. He probably told you."

"No," said Claire. "Not really. I knew he was angry. He thought he was being driven out of town."

"He was. My father had his own way of doing things. That was true after he died, too."

"But it wasn't your fault, Charlie."

Charlie looked away, toward the kitchen. "I know," he said. "But I felt guilty as hell about it. I hadn't done anything to deserve anything more than Owen. I didn't deserve to get all of it."

"I don't think Owen blamed you. He didn't talk about your father much. More when we first met. I thought he was scared of him."

"He was. We both were." Charlie shook his head. "He could be scary. Not as much near the end. He was real sick. And it seemed to mellow him out. Like he knew he was dying and he should try to make up for it. Something like that."

"People are funny."

"Yes. Yes, they are."

"You must miss Owen."

"I do. He was my best friend. But he won't come back here. This place would be too small for him now."

Claire smiled at him. "This was really nice."

Charlie looked down at their empty plates. "It was."

"I'll do the dishes," Claire said.

"No, let me."

"Don't even think about it. Have another glass of champagne. I'll be right back."

CHARLIE STOOD and went to the bar. He poured himself a snifter of cognac. The wind outside was howling now and he knew they were not going anywhere. He figured Claire knew this. The roads would be too dangerous.

When Claire returned Charlie poured her a cognac and they pulled their chairs up to the stove and they watched the fire. The light in the room was from the lamp over the bar and from the firebox and fingers of flame flickered up the tangerine walls. They both knew what was happening but neither of them knew how to begin it. Then Claire made the first move.

She leaned over and he sensed before he saw her and then her face was in front of his and she kissed him. Charlie kissed her back. She kissed him softly, and he kissed her back, and she felt his hands go to her face and she felt him holding her cheeks and she kissed him again. This time she tasted the liquor on his tongue and she stayed with it longer, reaching around the back of his head to move her fingers through his short hair. Charlie pulled back.

"Should we—" he said.

Claire put her finger over his mouth. "Don't," she said.

"I'm just—"

"Shush. Don't," Claire said. "Don't think."

Claire climbed into his lap and he held her with his strong arms, and she let him just hug her for a moment. Her hair was hanging in his face and she shook her head and with her hand she pushed the long bangs behind her ears. She moved in to kiss him again and this time they clanged teeth and Charlie said, "Sorry."

"It's okay. Slow, like this. No, wait," Claire said, pulling away. "I have an idea."

She left him and went into the kitchen. When she returned, her arms were full of table linens. "Help me," she said. "Let's make this floor bearable."

They carefully laid tablecloth after tablecloth down on the wide-plank hardwood. "That should work," Claire said when it was about twenty thick. "Lie with me, Charlie."

In the light from the woodstove they undressed and then they rolled together and they kissed, and when they made love, it was full of the uneasy movements of people together for the first time and Charlie told himself this and to relax. Claire was beautiful above him, though, and he watched her face, her closed eyes, her slightly open mouth.

They collapsed into each other. They rolled onto their backs and their breathing came fast and ragged. Claire looked up at the ceiling. There was an exposed beam above that she had never noticed before. Then again she had never had an occasion to lie on the floor of Charlotte's.

16

They slept that night on the floor of Charlotte's, covered with linens and an old blanket Charlie had found. They used stacks of napkins as pillows. Outside, the snow piled high against the building and in the morning the land would be transformed: drifting snow formed into great peaks on the flood-plain by the wind. Inside, things had changed as well and they both knew this though they did not give it words. In the weeks and months that followed, they simply gave in to it, into each other, though they did not tell anyone. They knew that the others might know. They sneaked kisses when no one was looking. They made less effort to get out of each other's way. That spring, Claire moved into the house on Signal Ridge, though she kept her apartment and returned there every few days for a change of clothes. It was a heady time and Charlie was in love and he had never been in love before. He hadn't known it meant you were warm all the time.

One night in early May they were lying in bed and they had just made love and Charlie was telling Claire about childhood trips they'd taken to the coast of Maine. Claire always marveled at how sex made the normally taciturn Charlie talkative. It was as if it turned on some valve and out came words and stories.

And Claire told him she had never been to Maine.

"You're kidding," said Charlie. He thought she had been everywhere.

"No. I haven't."

"We're going, then."

"When?"

"Right now," he said.

Claire laughed. "You're crazy."

"I'm serious. We'll get in the truck. Six hours and we're there."

"How about the morning? I want my sleep."

"Fine. The morning it is. I'll call Peg and Althea and the others."

"What are you going to say?"

"Gone fishing," said Charlie, and he laughed. Claire rolled into him and he held her.

IN THE morning they rose and Charlie called the waitresses and he asked Peg to call the reservations and reschedule them for later in the week. Peg asked him what was going on, and for the

first time, Charlie lied to her. He told her he was going to visit
his mother; that she was moving to a new place in the city and
needed his help. It was the only plausible story he could come
up with, and if Peg was skeptical she did not say so.

She said, "Tell Charlotte we all miss her."

"I will," said Charlie.

"You want me to call Claire and Joe?"

"You can call Joe. I'll tell Claire. I need to talk to her about
something else anyway."

"Okay, Charlie," said Peg.

An hour later, Charlie picked up Claire at her apartment,
where she had gone to pack a bag for the night. By ten o'clock
they were driving east out of town on the dirt roads and the day
was warm and they rode with the windows down. The sky above
was cloudless except for some high cirrus, brushstrokes next to
the sun. In the silence through which they drove, Charlie realized he was absolutely comfortable with her, more comfortable
than he had been with anyone in his life except his brother,
Owen, and he liked not having to talk. He liked the driving,
watching the road disappear under the tires of the truck, and he
liked the joy in knowing that he was about to give her something,
the coast of Maine, that she had never had before.

They crossed the Connecticut at noon, the river wide and blue
in the sunshine. The land flattened here, and they moved
through small towns on the rural highway, towns that looked like
stage sets on Western movies, facades of buildings a few blocks
long, and then a gas station and then back into the woods again.
Soon they entered the National Forest and the foothills rose in
front of them like great waves of green, Mount Washington,

craggy and gray standing above it all, sending descending cur-
tains of shadows down the hills below it.

The air grew cooler as they climbed in elevation and in front
of them were tourists towing trailers and driving slowly on the
winding roads but they did not care. The vistas stretched out in
all directions at the high parts on the two-lane and they could
see broad sweeps of green valley moving away from the mountains toward the north, toward Canada. Here and there they
could see white church steeples pointing out of the earth, re-
minders that not all of this country was forest, that down below
there were towns and people whose lives did not differ so much
from theirs.

Claire played with her long hair, absentmindedly twirling it
with her fingers. "It's nice not to be in a rush," she said.

"I know it," Charlie said. "No prep, right?"

"No prep," said Claire, and as she said it she turned and
smiled widely at him, reached over and put her hand on his
thigh, and squeezed.

IN TIME the mountains gave way to low-lying woods, white-water
brooks running along the side of the road, and then they saw the
sign that welcomed them to the state of Maine, and the roads
were instantly bumpy and ill-kempt, and the truck bounced as it
took the sharp turns through the birch forest that began right at
the roadside.

They drove through old mill towns and by dammed, fat rivers
and the air was rancid with the stink of rotting pulp. Men loi-

tered in convenience-store parking lots smoking cigarettes and wearing their despair like clothes. Midafternoon, they stopped at a roadside stand and they ate lobster rolls sitting on the hood of the truck. The lobster was fine and sweet and covered with mayonnaise and in a buttered hot dog roll and it was just what they wanted.

Then they were back in the car and it occurred to Claire that the road itself was no different from a river, moving down from the mountains and through the woods and, eventually, to the sea. There was an inexorableness to it, as if it knew where they were going better than they did themselves. At one point, when they were past Augusta and its confluence of rivers, she tried to express this to Charlie.

She said, "I can sense it."

"Sense what?"

"The ocean."

He laughed. "Okay," he said, and his tone was sarcastic when he said it and he immediately felt bad for it.

Claire reached out and lightly pushed him. "I'm serious," she said. "Does it ever strike you that the road is a river? That it moves toward the sea, only instead of emptying water there, it leaves us?"

Charlie looked at her with his pale blue eyes and he was going to make fun but he saw in her look that she was not messing around and so he smiled at her. "I like that," he said. "Roads like rivers. I see it."

THEY LEFT the forests behind as they approached the coast. The character of the land and the towns changed as well, the gritty hardscrabble life of western Maine giving way to small, gentrified postcard New England towns, towns built around churches and village greens. Towns with gourmet food shops and upscale restaurants.

"We're almost there," Charlie said.

"Where is there?"

"Camden," he said. "It was always my father's favorite town."

They came into Camden from the west, and Charlie chose this way because he did not want her to see the water until he was ready for her to, and soon they had reached Main Street and they drove past the stately old white homes and the large churches and Claire said, "Where's the ocean?"

"Can you smell it?"

The air was redolent with salt and brine. "Yes," she said, smiling. "I can."

"Right here," Charlie said, and he turned the truck into the harbor park and it appeared between the facades of buildings, the small harbor, full of white-sailed boats, a few small fishing trawlers. Beyond they could see the islands and then the blue green Atlantic, the horizon interrupted by large freighters like distant cities against the sky.

They parked the truck and climbed out. Claire was out first and she ran right to the seawall, stood on it and looked out at the boats bobbing on the soft chop, and the breeze was cool and smelled of salt and fish and the sun was warm on her arms.

"God, it's beautiful," said Claire.

"I know it."

"Let's walk out."

They followed the narrow seawall out the right side of the harbor and men on boats looked up from where they were working at the two of them moving like children along the top of the sea-wall. They passed the busy yacht club, a hotel where people sat on a veranda and looked out to the water, and when they reached the place where the few private homes started, they sat down and dangled their legs over the water. Soft waves slapped against the concrete below them. It was late afternoon and they watched the boat traffic moving into the harbor, sailboats mostly. They waved to the men and women on the boats. They leaned into each other. A few puffy clouds moved overhead in an otherwise crystal-clear blue ocean sky. Seagulls swept down over the harbor, their stark cries somehow, for Claire, completing the tableau, all of it feeling like a gift made especially for her, put together by a man whose strength she had known about, but whose generosity was starting to surprise her.

17

They rented a room at an old Victorian inn on High Street and the room took up the whole top floor of the house. Their four-poster bed was directly under the interior cone of a turret and it had small windows at its top and the afternoon light splashed across its walls when they lay down and made love. After, Claire took a bath in the Jacuzzi tub and Charlie stood and looked out the picture window at the harbor and beyond it to the ocean. The day was getting on and the sun had fallen lower in the sky. He watched the boat traffic move around the small islands and then in through the mouth of the harbor. Small fishing vessels dotted the ocean out past the islands. Against the horizon, as far off as he could see, were the thick grayish masses that were freighters, commercial vessels. Seeing them, Charlie thought of his brother.

It had been six years now since he had seen Owen. The post-cards still came with regularity, but there was something re-markably impersonal about a postcard. For one, everyone could read them and so they never said anything important. Second, there was no way for Charlie to respond—it was as if his brother, from whatever corner of the globe he was in, was holding his hand out, palm toward Charlie, and saying, You have your life, let me have mine. This card is simply my way of showing you I am still here. And that you can't find me.

Charlie knew that his own life had gone on as it should, with the exception of Claire. Not much had changed and he knew that Owen, who now lived on ships, would see it that way. But what would he think of him and Claire? Of the small changes in the restaurant? What would he make of the once-in-fifty-years flood that had almost taken everything away? Where was he? Was he out on the blue green Atlantic, standing on the deck of some massive boat against the horizon, looking toward the room in which Charlie stood?

Standing in the window of the old inn, listening to Claire mov-ing around in bathwater behind the thick wooden door, looking out at the great freighters at the edge of the world, Charlie sud-denly longed for his brother. He longed to share his life with him again, to have someone who understood him in a way that no one ever could, not even Claire; someone to hear him out, to help him make sense of it all, in the way that only brothers are capa-ble of doing.

———

AFTER CLAIRE had bathed and dressed, they left the inn and walked back toward the harbor. Claire and Charlie held hands as they walked. The sun was starting to fall behind the Camden Hills to the west, and the sea breeze was cool even though it was warm for early May, and Claire moved into Charlie, letting go of his hand and moving into him, hooking her arm into his, and she liked the way she imagined they looked to others, wearing the badge of new lovers for all to see, none of the secrecy they had taken on back at Charlotte's.

They ate at a small café that overlooked the harbor and the hostess seemed surprised that they wanted to eat on the deck since it was so early in the season.

"We're Vermonters," Charlie said by way of explanation. "We'll be fine."

They drank a bottle of Chardonnay and they watched the sailboats, the water in the harbor darkening as the sun set and as the outline of the pale moon rose over the town.

Soon the lights on the sailboats came on as the darkness grew, illuminated masts rising out of the water, like Christmas trees in May. The wine was going to their heads. Everything suddenly effervescent and good. Claire, looking out over the water from the deck, at the boats and the harbor and the town beyond it, let her eyes linger on all of it before turning them back to Charlie. She ran her foot up his leg and he smiled at her. She returned the smile and neither of them needed to say anything.

Back at the inn, they made love on the floor of their room and it was a thick carpet and in the morning they would both have rug burns on their knees but they did not care. After, they showered together and they were drunk and they knew it but they did not care about this either. Charlie stood behind Claire while the water ran over them and he wrapped his arms around her and under her breasts and the water spilled off both of them and then fell to the porcelain tub bottom at their feet.

They climbed under the sheets and their hair was still wet and they were naked and cold and they rolled into each other for warmth. Charlie went to sleep first, and when he did he fell away from Claire, and though the alcohol had gone to her head she was curiously full of energy and could not sleep. She lay and listened to the comfort of his snores, loud and steady, falling the way they did when he had drunk too much, all of it coming up and through his nose. Then she rose and stood and walked to the window. She looked through herself until she could make out the lighthouse at the point, its beam moving rhythmically across the small sound. She watched it until she could not watch anymore. Until she felt her eyes grow heavy. Then she climbed back under the now-warm sheets, slid her body next to Charlie's, and dreamed of ocean waves crashing against the large stones of a jetty.

IN THE morning they checked out of the inn and ate breakfast in town. Then they drove back to Eden and got there in time to open for that evening. For another month they kept their relationship secret, or at least thought they were keeping it secret, though it grew harder since the trip to Maine had drawn them closer together.

Inside the kitchen of Charlotte's they might not have fooled anyone about the truth of their relationship, but if anyone noticed how it affected what they did when they were working they did not point it out. And it was as if their lovemaking at the house on Signal Ridge somehow found its way into the cooking taking place in front of the stove. They relaxed into each other's creativity; they pushed each other in new ways, experimenting with new ideas, some that worked, others that did not, all of them, though, helping to elevate Charlotte's to levels of excellence it had never seen before. Charlie was motivated as he had not been since his father died. He wanted, through all his actions, to fill Claire with wonder, to show her what he could do. All that mattered to him was Claire, what she thought, how she liberated him to do what he wanted. For the first time in his life he felt unshackled from the past, as if the ghost of his father, of his life before he met her, was disappearing into the shadows and no one could recall it but himself.

He wanted to show her everything. He wanted her to know all that he knew.

Once he took her to a place he had not been since he was a child, a place his father had taken him and Owen to show them what he considered the most magical thing in all of Eden. It was something they did for a number of years in a row when they were just boys and he did not know why they stopped going. Perhaps, he thought, it was because they outgrew it; though he knew when he took Claire there that it could not have been true. For when, he asked himself afterward, do we become too old for beauty?

It was the end of May, and a Friday, and though it was expected to be a busy night at the restaurant, Charlie said the prep could wait. They drove in the morning under blue skies through Eden, past Main Street, into the old village, and then up the sloping hill to where the glacial footprint of Mirror Lake sat between steep forest walls of spruce.

At the southern end of Mirror Lake, across from the old Fiske house, was a small stream that was unknown to those outside of Eden, a stream that ran through a cove and then out of the tooth-shaped lake and that was, in fact, the headwaters of the Dog River. They parked on the side of the road and they walked to the lake's edge. In the windless morning the lake was as still as glass. Charlie did not tell Claire where he was taking her, and she did not mind, for he had also not told her anything when he showed her where to forage for the chanterelles on the forest floor; and as a result she trusted him to lead her to something she could not discover on her own; something she would want to see.

They walked in silence. They followed the shore of the lake to the small peninsula that jutted out and was filled with scrub trees. The cold of the night was burning off and the day was suddenly warm. At the mouth of the stream Charlie said, "This way," and they entered the woods to their right, moving gingerly along the banks of the small stream.

Though the stream was narrow, it was deep and the water was muddy and filled with silt and they could not see the bottom. Near its first bend, they flushed a wild turkey from some heavy brush and it was visible for a moment, waddling in front of them, before it vanished into the darkness of the deep green forest.

"That would have been some good eating," Charlie said.

"Not the season, is it?"

"No, not until fall."

The land began to climb here, a gradual sloping upward, and they walked again in silence. As they went up the hill, the trees grew closer together and the going was slower. The undergrowth was heavy and for a time they had to move away from the stream, for the banks of it were impassable. Soon though the growth gave way to a hard forest floor and they made better time. They caught up to the stream again, and it was on their right now, below them, a drop of about four feet to the dark water.

"Almost there," said Charlie.

The stream in front of them meandered to the right through a grove of trees. They beelined to where it bent back, and when they reached it Charlie said, "Look."

Claire looked up. In front of her was a waterfall, falling perhaps seven feet into a deep pool. Above it, thin birches grew and their bark looked silvery in the sunlight filtering through the canopy above. The tumbling water frothed and foamed as it fell.

"It's beautiful," said Claire.

Charlie smiled. "You haven't seen the half of it. Come on."

He took her hand then, and they jogged toward the pool, stepping over thick roots and small bushes on the ground below. When they reached the edge of the pool, Claire saw that it was lined with granite, and they stood only a few feet from the waterfall and when the cold spray reached them it dampened their shirts.

"I love it," Claire said.

"Look," said Charlie, pointing toward the water.

Claire looked and she saw the water churning and not just from the sharp current where the waterfall met the pool. Underneath the surface she could see them, large shadowy shapes.

"What are they?"

"Steelhead," said Charlie. "Rainbows. Or they will be. Later. Now watch."

Claire watched as first one and then another long, slender fish, slightly speckled, left the water in front of her eyes, giant graceful leaps toward the heart of the swift water above, their bodies flying straight like tiny planes. One after another they hit the outcropping of rock where the water began its plunge, and one after another they fell back into the pool.

"They're not making it," Claire cried.

"Don't worry," Charlie said. "They will."

And as he said it, one large fish propelled itself out of the water, landed where the others had, only this time she saw its silver tail kick and it sat almost still for an instant, the water running over its sleek body, and then it was almost as if it were pulled forward, inexorably, shooting upstream as fast as smoke.

They stayed there for an hour and they did not talk. They sat on a mossy log and they listened to the sound of the falls and they watched the steelhead on their annual migration.

18

About a week later, Charlie rolled over one morning in bed to find Claire gone. Out the window he could see that the sun was already high in the sky. He had slept longer than he normally did. He shook the grogginess of sleep from his head and half sat up in the bed. It was then that he saw her through the open door of the bathroom. She had just showered, and she wore a towel around her waist like a man would, and her breasts were naked to him, and from the profile she presented to him he could see their slight upward curve, and her belly below, and he saw where the towel ended and her thigh tapered to her knee; and he could see how she looked at herself in the mirror as she combed the tangles out of her long hair, tilting her head first to the right and then to the left, running the brush through it. She was still wet from the shower and the bare skin of her shoulders glistened with water. She had no idea he was watching her. Charlie thought: I could watch her forever. Just like this. And as he thought it, she turned and saw him watching her, and she smiled at him, as if she was privy to the arc of his thoughts.

"Hey, sleepy," she said.

Charlie climbed out of bed and she giggled as she watched him walk toward her, and he realized he was half-hard but he did not care. He entered the bathroom and Claire saw the way he was looking at her, his face full of intent, and she said, "What?"

Charlie fell to his knees in front of her, and with this supplication he ran his hands up over her towel, up toward her breasts, and he looked up at her. He turned his head to the side for a moment and hugged her legs, the way a child would, and then he turned back and looked up at her.

"Marry me, Claire," he said. "Marry me."

Claire laughed. She shook her hair and water spilled off it and landed on him. "You're crazy."

"I'm serious," he said. "Look at me."

And as he said it, the corners of his icy blue eyes grew wet and she knew he was serious, that he was dead serious.

"Do you know what you're doing, Charlie Bender?"

"I want you to be my wife, Claire Apple."

Claire shook her head again. Charlie saw her gulp hard. "I don't believe this, it's been like five months."

"I don't care, when you know, you know. And I know this. I don't ever want to spend a moment away from you if I can help it. Ah, shit. I'm no good at this, Claire, help me out. I don't know what to say. I'm dying here."

"Okay," she said.

"Okay?"

"Yes," she said. "Yes, Charlie. I will marry you."

"Say it again."

"I will marry you."

"Shout it," said Charlie.

"I will marry you," Claire shouted, and now the tears ran freely over her high cheekbones, and Charlie rose to his feet and he picked her up in his arms and he leaned back and held her, and then he put her down and she kissed him hard on the mouth, and he kissed her back, and then he held her and he realized that she was shaking, and he wrapped his arms around her as much as he could, doing everything possible to keep her warm.

19

Some mornings that summer, she woke after the heat had already risen, and lying nude next to Charlie she could feel his warm skin next to hers and her thoughts almost always turned to the creeping shadow of doubt that the sobriety of this time of day gave her. There was something about the morning, with the long day in front of her, that made her anxious, allowed her to doubt what they intended to do, allowed her to doubt the coming marriage. She knew that these were ephemeral thoughts; that by the afternoon they would be all but gone and that by the evening she would find herself wondering how she had thought them at all. But they came to her, and the fact that they did alarmed her, and she told herself as she felt him against her that she needed to address them. If only for herself.

It was not that she didn't love Charlie, for she thought she did; and it was not that she did not want to marry him, for she thought this was true as well; it was more a feeling she could not place, a creeping dread, something that she suspected was particular to her, an insecurity perhaps, a flaw, but not something that could actually be true to them. She told herself that if she willed it away it would go. But still it persisted.

While he snored next to her, she thought of all the reasons she loved this man. There were his eyes for one. Icy blue and translucent, she adored how they fixed on her, inscrutable and yet all-knowing at the same time. There was his height, his strength, the way he carried himself. He walked with humility and confidence at the same time: it was almost like he knew himself, what he was good at, but he was also wise enough to know that he should be without arrogance. And there was his cooking, his quiet grace in the kitchen, the best she had ever seen, born to it, with instinct and talent, creativity and a sharp understanding of all that had gone before him. He knew what should be done and then he executed it and he never questioned himself. He did not look back.

Most of all there was how he related to her; how he looked at her; how he seemed incapable of suppressing his desire for her. He made her feel wanted and sometimes she thought that that was all any woman wanted, and when she found it, she had an obligation to hang on to it.

Still, her own behavior mystified her. After he proposed to her in the bathroom that morning, Claire felt something come over her like a rush of heat, something ineluctable, and she could not describe it but it made her want to crawl under the comforter on the big bed and stay there and sleep. Charlie, by contrast, was ebullient, picking her up and whirling her around the room, and he wanted to immediately tell everyone that they were engaged. And he did not want to wait to get married, initially even talking about doing it right away, showing up at the town hall on Monday with Joe Collins and Peg and her parents as witnesses, getting it done.

But she succeeded, at least, in convincing him to hold off until the fall, until they could plan something. She had not even told her parents yet about Charlie, beyond telling them that he was talented and was good to work for.

She sat in bed on the morning he had proposed and she pulled her knees up to her chest and she listened to him on the phone, talking to his mother, a woman she had not seen since she was in high school, and she wanted to be touched by the words he used as he told her how happy he was, how much he was in love, how beautiful and smart and talented Claire—his fiancée, a new word, as foreign as Greek to her ears—was. And when he was done, he wanted to know if she wanted to call her parents, and when she said she needed to wait, he looked puzzled, and she could not stop herself. She started to cry.

"What is it?" he said.

"It's nothing."

Charlie sat down on the bed next to her. "You're crying."

"It's nothing. It's me."

"Okay," he said.

"I'll be okay," she said. "I will." She managed a thin smile. "I'm just a little scared, that's all."

Charlie pushed her hair away from her face, and then he stood up, and he left, and when he returned he did not speak, though he handed her a cup of herbal tea, and she realized he seemed to know when to leave her alone, and when to be present; and he seemed to know what it was that she needed without her having to say anything. Claire knew enough about men to know that his ability to read her was exceptional, and that she should be more grateful for it.

SUMMER IN Eden is both glorious and short. The days themselves are long and languid, sometimes tropically hot, other times as cool as fall, so that at night when you sit on the porch you need a sweater. The muted golden green of spring gives way to lush rain-forest-like growth everywhere. The rivers run fat and lazy. The sunsets over the mountains are brilliant on clear days, bright pink turning to red and then to purple as the moon rises through the color and the stars appear suddenly, millions of them, their light growing with each passing hour.

In the kitchen of Charlotte's, the heat was often unbearable. Some nights it would be in the eighties outside, but over a hundred in front of the stove and the grill, the water that always seemed to be boiling on the range filling the air with moisture it did not need. At the end of a busy night, Charlie and Claire would be soaked with sweat, and on some of these evenings, after everyone else had left, they went out back and in the dark they crossed the floodplain to the Dog River, where, lit only by the moon, they would strip off their clothes and wade into the cool mountain water, sitting down on smooth rocks beneath the surface, the soft current swirling around them, the black woods all around them, another day passed.

————

THEY WERE married in September of that year. Claire's parents
came over for dinner on a Sunday night when a soft summer rain
fell. He did not go out of his way to impress them, grilling veal
chops over a wood fire. He decided to be himself and it seemed
to work, for Claire was nervous about it, and said so; she inti-
mated that her parents were reluctant supporters of their decision. He knew them, of course, but only as customers, and in the
roundabout way everyone in a small town knew one another.

Still, spending time with them as their future son-in-law, he
discovered he liked them. He could not help it. They were
Claire's parents and in each of them he saw her. Her mother had
her dark eyes, her tumble of black hair. She was in her fifties and
Charlie thought she was a very attractive woman, even if she
seemed wary of him. Her father had the firm handshake and de-
meanor of the corporate executive he was, but he also had a soft
smile, lines coming off his mouth at the corners, as they did on
Claire when she laughed.

After her parents left, they were in the kitchen, cleaning up,
when Claire suddenly leaned up and kissed him.

"I love you, Charlie Bender," she said.

"I love you, too," he said.

Her face was aglow. "I mean it, thank you."

"What for? I didn't do anything."

"For being you," she said. "For being nice to my parents."

"Of course I was nice to your parents," he said with a shrug.

"No 'of course' about it," said Claire. "You were great. I mean
that."

"So the wedding is on?" he asked jokingly.

"Yes," she said, leaning up and kissing him again, resting her hand on his broad chest. "The wedding is on."

A WEEK before the wedding and still no word from Owen. Charlotte was coming from New York along with some of her friends from way back, Sam Marsh and the others who were there at the birth of the restaurant. Charlotte had not heard from Owen either, except for the postcards which came faithfully to her door, too. She did not know what to tell Charlie and he did not expect her to tell him anything. But he was getting married and he wanted his brother to be there. One day in a life, he thought. That is all I ask.

He called the union offices for the Merchant Marines in Boston and in New York. In Boston no one knew the name, and while in New York the second guy he talked to did know Owen, he had not seen him for months.

"Last time I saw him he was waiting for a ship," the man said.

"Waiting for a ship?"

"Yeah. I'm guessing he got it because I haven't seen him."

Charlie gave up hope that his brother would make it and got down to the business of making this wedding go.

Claire and Charlie decided, after much deliberation, to cater the event themselves. It was going to be a small wedding, around forty people, and they knew that they were the only ones in the area who could do precisely what they wanted.

Two days before the ceremony, they made their wedding cake. They worked all day and deep into the night, baking round after round of cake, renting a massive mixer for the different frostings, using more than a hundred eggs in the process. It was warm in the kitchen, and by the time they had assembled the large tiered cake, constructing it with wooden dowels that held it all together, it was after midnight, and they were focused but drunk on sherry, covered with flour, and more than a little sweaty from the exertion of the work.

When they finished they stood back and looked at it, two and a half feet high, a thing of beauty, Charlie said, and they collapsed into each other with exhaustion.

They swam in the river that night, and then slept on the floor of the restaurant as they had during the blizzard, and when they moved together they did so wearily, still wet from the cool water, and afterward they dozed off in a half hug, before Charlie fell away, onto his back, Claire slinging her arm across his chest.

The morning of the wedding they cooked a dinner they could serve at room temperature. They poached whole sockeye salmon in white wine and fresh herbs. They roasted a beef tenderloin and let it rest before slicing it thinly. They made a horseradish sauce to go with it. They made a large salad of fresh tomatoes, basil, and goat cheese. They blanched green beans and tossed them with olive oil, tarragon, shallots, and lemon juice. They made nori rolls filled with smoked tuna to pass before dinner.

When they finished cooking, Charlie kissed Claire good-bye and stayed at the restaurant until Joe Collins arrived with a borrowed van to take all the food, and most delicately, the cake, up to the house on Signal Ridge. After Joe had gone, Charlie walked outside and he stopped for a moment before getting into his truck to drive to the house and change into his suit, prepare to get married. It was a perfect day, just what he wanted. A deep blue sky, lazy, fat clouds moving past the mountains. The forest was still green; the first leaves had not started to change. He looked down the valley, toward Hunger Mountain. A red-tailed hawk made wide circles above the spruce trees. A light comfortable breeze rustled his shirt. He breathed in deep, closed his eyes, and looked toward the sun, orange and yellow streaks on the back of his eyelids.

20

Charlie wore a crisp white shirt with a vest over it, no tie, black pants. He stood under the arbor next to the Reverend Smith. Reverend Smith, now eighty, and mostly blind, wore a baby blue jacket, a thin black tie, Coke-bottle glasses. He jokingly called himself the marrying man, for since he had retired after thirty years at the Methodist church in Eden village, he had done little but marry the youth of Eden and drink the brandy he made from his blueberry patch. He rocked slowly back and forth, clutching a worn and aged Bible in his hands. In front of him, Charlie surveyed the guests, all seated in white rental chairs. In the front row was his mother, on her right was Sam Marsh. To the left of her the seat was empty, as if deliberately, as if Owen might show up at the last minute and fill it.

Charlotte sat there and emanated strength; for Charlie knew this was difficult for her, being back in Eden, being back in the house she had shared with her husband, and he also knew that she would never admit to it. To his right, and a little behind him, a woman from town whom Claire had found softly played classical guitar.

They were in a field behind the house, what had once been an apple orchard under previous owners, and a few of the gnarly small trees were still present, though they had long ago stopped yielding fruit. Below them was the house, and beyond it he could see the woods where he'd grown up hunting and where his father had ended his life.

Charlie held his hands behind his back and he looked at the house below him, and he watched the cow path that ran along its side and he thought: Any moment now. Any moment now she will round that bend and this will become real. And no sooner had he thought it than he saw the dark brown of the horse, and then it emerged into the opening, and he saw her and her father on a wagon behind it. A murmur went up through the crowd and all eyes turned toward where his already rested. The old wagon they were in made its way up the path toward the ceremony, and from where he stood Charlie could see it swaying slightly as it negotiated the rutted old road. Soon they were close enough for him to see Claire, and she wore her mother's wedding dress, which she had told him she would do, though he had not seen it. Her thick curly hair was piled high on her head and she was wearing makeup, though she had never done so for him before, and when they reached the edge of where everyone sat, and her father pulled on the reins and brought the big chestnut horse to a stop, Charlie got his first good look at her and he felt something give within himself. I would die for her, he thought. If I had to, I would die for her.

Claire's father stepped out of the wide bench seat of the antique wagon and walked around it and held his hand out for his daughter. Claire took his hand and smiled wanly out toward the guests and she stepped down. Together they began to walk, toward the back rows, and in that instant everyone stood from where they sat and watched her as she went and the guitar player played with greater intensity now and Charlie took his eyes off his future wife for a moment to make sure that Reverend Smith knew what was happening.

At that moment, the reverend's eyes opened behind his thick glasses and his head swiveled toward where Claire was now moving behind the last row of chairs, arms locked with her father, preparing to make her way down what passed for an aisle.

As they entered the aisle, Charlie turned and faced the audience, faced Claire, and for a moment they locked eyes and she seemed to smile at him, though he knew she was all nerves now; he could see it in her face, and he thought that he should be, too, though he was curiously calm, everything slowing down for him with each step she took closer to where he stood.

Claire and her father marched slowly, conscious of the ritual, and the guitar played plaintively, and to Charlie it seemed to take forever. Soon they made it, reached to where he stood, and Claire's father leaned down and gave her a kiss on the cheek, before letting go. Before he went to his seat, he stopped and shook Charlie's hand, and his smile as he did so was wide and warm and Charlie smiled back at him, thankful to him for all that smile imparted.

The reverend began to speak. Slow, incantatory words, and in truth later neither Charlie nor Claire would remember anything he had said. He spoke of love and he spoke of marriage and he spoke of family and he spoke of the land. He closed his eyes when he spoke, and he rocked back on his heels and he raised his arms to the sky and the words were good words but Charlie and Claire were both fixated on each other, on each other's eyes. When he said to repeat after me, they did; when he said to exchange rings, they did, Charlie taking both of them out of the breast pocket of his shirt, handing his to Claire to put on his finger while he slid the simple gold band onto hers. And when he said you can now kiss the bride, Charlie said, not fully realizing until the moment had passed that it was out loud, "It's about time."

Behind him he heard the laughter, and some clapping, and he went to his bride and he took her into his arms, leaned her back away from him, and under the arbor he kissed her, harder than he probably should have; and when he pulled her back up, they turned and faced the crowd, bright faces with the woods behind them, the sound washing over them, the guitar, the reverend, the clapping of everyone else.

IN FRONT of the house there was a large tent and under it were tables, and before dinner the guests huddled in groups and talked and drank champagne out of large, stemless flutes. Peg and Althea, though they were guests, took the time to pass the nori rolls, refresh people's drinks. Joe Collins laid the food on a buffet table, and a three-piece fiddle band set up a mock stage behind the wooden dance floor. The afternoon was warm and many of the men took off their jackets.

Claire and Charlie walked from group to group, her arm locked in his, and they accepted the congratulations of all. Charlotte gave Claire a big hug, and when she looked up at Charlie her eyes wrinkled and her mouth parted with a show of pride and happiness.

There was no best man, so before they ate, Charlie rose from his seat to speak. He raised his glass of champagne and everyone else did as well. He was not normally given to eloquence but today he found it within himself. He thanked everyone for coming. He talked about what it meant to him. He told them that he had found in Claire what he had always been looking for. Someone to share his life with, his vision, his love of food, and this hillside he loved.

Charlie smiled. "There are two people missing today, and I hope that somewhere they know what is happening in this field. One of course is my father, who I know we all miss tremendously. And the other is my brother, Owen, who will always be welcome in my life, wherever he is. I ask that you raise your glasses to Claire and me, but I also ask that you raise them to Owen, too. And while you're at it, spill a little on the ground for my father."

"Hear, hear," someone shouted, and everyone drank long and fast from the champagne, leaving a little in the glass which they dumped onto the grassy lawn at their feet.

"Let's eat," said Charlie.

They lined up and brought their food back to the tables and they ate. The food was just what they needed for this weather, the tender beef, the rich poached salmon. They drank wine, and after, they danced. Charlie and Claire took the first turn, and then Charlie danced with his mother while Claire danced with her father. The fiddle band picked it up, playing hard and fast, and many of the guests took to the floor, bodies moving in the late-afternoon sunlight.

Soon the afternoon bled into evening, and the guests gathered outside the tent to watch the September sunset. It fell behind the hills, and after it was gone a tapestry of red stayed in the sky, before fading to dark. Some people left but most stayed and the wine flowed. At nine o'clock, Joe Collins brought the horse and wagon around, and this time it was Charlie who would ride with Claire on it. The band stopped and the guests gathered to see them off. Claire threw her bouquet now, and it disappeared into the darkness for a moment before coming down into the waiting hands of Charlotte herself.

"Claire," Charlotte shouted. "What am I supposed to do with this?"

Claire smiled and shrugged, and Charlie gave a big wave and pulled on the reins, and the horse began its slow clop away from the tent. Above, in the sky, it had started on the far western horizon, moving toward Signal Ridge. At first it looked like bright starlight, but as it grew, there were different colors, greens and reds and shades of gold against the black firmament. Soon it covered the whole sky, the first time the northern lights had been visible in Eden for almost ten years. They were like great arms, pulsing with color, and now that Charlie and Claire had ridden away for a night at the inn, the guests who were left lay down on the dewy grass and stared up at the sky, all eyes on the celestial event above.

21

Shortly after they were married, Claire felt that she suddenly knew what it was all about. Rolling over in the mornings and seeing Charlie there, and then working together as husband and wife, all of it hers now, too, she felt a comfort and a warmth from the certainty of it all. She loved their mornings together, the coffee they shared with the paper, and she loved the daily drive to Charlotte's, cutting through those old dirt roads, the windows rolled up in the winter, days when she would move close to her husband on the bench seat of the pickup truck and watch the snowy woods that they passed through. Summer mornings when they drove with the windows down, the warm breeze entering the cab, the whole world bright and full of possibility. Mostly, though, she loved the restaurant itself, the bustle and noise of it, more than a job now, more than work to mark time, but a life, a life that belonged to both of them.

And then, their first spring as a married couple, a spring when the melt came early and steadily and the days grew gradually warmer and longer, her favorite time of year, she discovered that she was pregnant. Oddly, it was not something they had spoken of much. There were drunken talks about the idea of children, what they would look like. Would they have his height, her eyes? How would it work, bringing them into the life of a restaurant, a job that never ended?

But, unlike most married couples, they did not plan for it. It was not something they talked about in a concrete way, as other young married women Claire had known discussed it. In the third year, we will have our first, and then one each year after until we hit the magic number of three. No, there was none of that. It remained an abstraction, something that happened to other people, though deep within both of them they probably understood that this was denial, that by their decision to not use birth control, relying instead on Charlie's ability to end things when he chose, they were relinquishing some authority over the choice of it all.

Claire knew her period was late. For a brief time she thought perhaps it was only that and she did not say anything to Charlie. Since she had been back in Eden, her cycle had been in perfect alignment with the full moon, as regular as a clock. When one week passed she began to think about it, and when two weeks passed she began to worry about it. One morning she left the restaurant on the pretense of going to the bank and she drove out of town and found a drugstore where the clerks did not know her and she bought one of the instant pregnancy tests they had for sale next to the cigarettes and the condoms. She waited until that night, and while Charlie slept soundlessly she took the test.

The results were not unexpected. She was pregnant. She did not tell Charlie right away. Somehow she hoped that if she did not give it words it would not come to pass. And she knew this was the wrong way to think but she could not help it. A child threatened the life she had grown to love so much: just the two of them, the restaurant, the work, the freedom.

She waited until Sunday morning, until the one day they did not have to rise early and head to Charlotte's. She woke before him that day, and outside the late April sun was already bright. She had played this conversation over in her mind, what she would tell him, but when he finally stirred next to her, raised his arms above his head and smiled at her, rolling half over and slinging his arm across her belly, all she could say was, "I'm pregnant."

Charlie quickly sat up. "My God. Really?"

Claire nodded. "I'm pretty sure."

"Ah, Claire," he said. "That's wonderful."

Claire smiled thinly. She looked out the window to the green woods, to the high clouds in the sky. "It is," she said, her voice betraying her lack of enthusiasm.

"What?" said Charlie. "This is great news. I mean, it's not something we planned for. But still. It's amazing."

Claire saw how his eyes lit up, and she thought, How do I explain it? How do I tell him why this makes me so uneasy? How do I tell him how afraid I am? And as she thought this, he moved into her, put his strong arms around her body, and pulled her to him. She felt his lips on her neck and the stubble of his beard scraped the side of her cheek.

He said, "I love you, Claire."

"I love you, too," she said.

"This will be amazing, honest. It will."

Claire nodded her head, and she wanted to tell him what she thought, that she was not cut out to be a mother; that some girls were, it was what they wanted from the time they were old enough to think about such things. She was not one of them, she knew that. She figured she was too selfish. Cared too much about her own life to throw everything she had into nurturing the life of another. And she hated herself for this, for what kind of woman did not welcome the coming of a child to a man she was married to? A man she loved? What kind of woman did not put a child above a job? Though she knew that was not fair either. Charlotte's was not simply a job, cooking was not simply a job. It was a life. But she could not tell him this. She could never tell Charlie this. So she simply returned his hug. She dug her hands into his back. She looked out the window to the broad valley below. To the hills and the mountains and the sun in the sky. To all that lay beyond her.

AND THEN with the full acknowledgment of it, the uncertainty gave way to love, love for what grew within her. In the soft nights of spring the two of them lay together in bed and they talked about names, boy names and girl names, and they talked about things that they had not realized were of import to either of them but that the prospect of a child suddenly made real. They talked about religion, and the truth was that neither of them was religious, Charlie being raised in a secular house and Claire as a

Lutheran but not practicing since high school. They talked about school, about the possibility of homeschooling, which had never occurred to Claire until she began to think about it, picturing in her mind her son or daughter coming home from some Vermont public school unhappy and unsatisfied, remembering her own unhappiness years ago in junior high, the relentless teasing of a girl whose breasts were prematurely large and whose beauty had not yet become objectively apparent. They talked about all these things, and in the talking she found herself reaching a level of comfort that mirrored the physical changes within her, the growing baby, the new heft to her tummy, the sense of motherhood that seemed to cover all of her, the general warmth of it, the feeling of strength it gave her. And for this, she loved Charlie more and more, and in the shared sense of future that only a child can provide, she saw the two of them growing closer together, as if they were old vines climbing the clapboards of a house.

Early in the pregnancy, she was sick, not in the mornings as she expected, but mostly in the middle of the night, waking and moving quickly to the bathroom, where she retched into the toilet. If Charlie heard her, he rose, too, and came to her, held her head, soothed her with his words. Sometimes she grew unfathomably emotional, stealing downstairs in the dead of night to be away from him to a place where she could sob in peace. But mostly, she learned to adjust to the change, and by the time she was six months along, her body full of the baby to come, her cheeks flushed with it, she knew she was ready. Ready for the birth, desiring it, and ready for the life to follow. For how their lives would change, for she knew enough to know that a baby could not help but change people.

Those last months she worked whenever she felt up to it, and they never talked about it but Claire knew that Charlie would prefer that she did not but he was wise enough not to suggest such a thing. She went to Charlotte's in the mornings and she prepped for the night's dinner, sitting on a stool rather than standing up. In the afternoons she returned home and napped and came back for the rush of dinner, though she did not work the line as she once had. She admired how good Charlie was in the kitchen on these days, for he was doing the work of two and made it seem effortless. She watched him move from stove to grill and back again, as many as twelve entrées going at any given time, and all of it coming out just as it should. He took the time in the chaos of things to turn and smile at her, to mouth the words *I love you*. And sometimes when he did this, she felt herself overcome by it, and she knew it was the pregnancy, how it made you aware of the simplest of gestures, how it made you understand their greater human import, and she smiled at him.

Winter came late again that year. By December there was still no snow on the ground, though the earth had hardened and on the roads the grooves left over from the previous spring were now frozen ridges that jolted the truck as it went and made Claire uncomfortable. Her official due date was December 13. The baby could come any day now. Both she and Charlie were uneasy about it. If they were to speak of it, perhaps they would recognize that the life of the restaurant was one of rigid control: you did everything you could to manage the future. And they both knew, of course, that babies arrive when babies arrive, and that there was not much use in expecting otherwise. Still, lying in bed as midnight passed and the thirteenth came, Claire turned to Charlie and said, "It's not going to happen today."

He rubbed his eyes and rolled toward her. He had just started to doze off. "How do you know?"

"I don't know. I just do. It's going to be a Christmas baby."

Charlie laughed. "Okay," he said. "There are worse things to get in your stocking than a new baby."

"Christmas it is then," said Claire.

"Christmas it is," Charlie said.

AS IT turned out, the baby came on December 23. They had had plenty of opportunities to learn the sex and did not, one of the things they both agreed on, deciding to be old-fashioned about it. And if they had a preference, they did not express it to each other. Claire secretly hoped for a boy, and she thought she knew it was a boy, not that she had any way to know, but something about the weight within her, the way the baby moved in those weeks before birth suggested to her a little boy.

And then, that morning, she woke and knew it was happening. She felt it and she did not have to have experienced it before to know that this was no fire drill, the pain was hot and white and in her abdomen, and when she calmed her breathing the contractions were fast and regular.

Charlie was in the bathroom shaving. In a few moments, as he did every morning now that she did not join him at Charlotte's, he would kiss her good-bye and get in the truck and drive the snowy roads to the restaurant. Claire felt the pain.

"Charlie?" she called. No answer. Again. Louder. "Charlie?" And then even louder, practically screaming it. "Charlie!"

The door to the bathroom opened and he was there, shaving cream on his face, a towel around his waist, her tall, muscular husband. She almost did not have to speak for she saw in his face that he knew. But she said it anyway. She said, "It's happening."

He removed his towel, wiped the shaving cream off his face, and at the same time said repeatedly, "Okay, okay."

Claire tried to rise from the bed but the pain was intense and she lay back down. The pain was so strong she felt the first tears of the day come to her eyes. The room around her grew blurry. She had a sense of Charlie's frenetic movements, his sliding into jeans, his buttoning of his shirt, his rummaging through his closet for his boots. Then, somehow, she was in the truck and her hands were on the turbulence that was her belly, and they were driving, Charlie's words distant but soothing, nothing more than his incessant *okays* but they helped nonetheless.

Soon they were leaving Eden. She knew he was driving fast, could feel the road vanishing beneath the tires of the truck. And then they were at Copley Hospital, bright lights, people taking care of her, Charlie fading into the background except for his strong hand which refused to let go of her own.

"It'll be okay, baby," he said to her.

Later she would remember the midwife, a round-faced woman with curly hair and a broad smile. And she would remember the doctor who came in to oversee things, gray-bearded and blue-eyed. And she would remember Charlie, more nervous than she had ever seen him before, his face the color of flour, his eyes furtive and darting. What she would not remember was the pain,

that flowed easily up the grate to the bedroom. Charlie was downstairs and she could hear him making her tea, the whistle of the kettle before he turned it off. And she wanted to cry, not out of sadness but because of what it all meant, the two of them, and the baby who in only a few days had already become more a part of her than he had been when he rested within her.

By the time Charlie brought her the mug of warm herbal tea, little Jonah was done feeding and slept soundlessly on the lip of her chest, his little rib cage rising and falling with each tiny breath.

Claire said, "Look, Charlie. Look at this boy we made."

Charlie smiled wide, leaned down, and kissed her forehead. "I know it," he said.

"I can't believe it," Claire whispered.

"Believe it, Claire," Charlie said. "It's just the beginning." And with that, he kissed her forehead again, reached down and held his big hand over the head of his baby boy, as if he was going to cup the bowl of his skull, instead holding it there for an instant before taking her free hand in his own and squeezing tight. He smiled at her and she smiled back and outside the short day moved on toward dark.

JONAH WAS a healthy boy and he grew like a tree. Each day of motherhood brought new joys and new challenges and Claire surprised herself by how easily she moved into it. When she expressed this to Charlie one night with the baby upstairs asleep, the steady tick of the baby monitor on the table next to where they sat, he said, "See? You're a natural."

Claire looked at him. "I really didn't think I had it in me," she said. "It's not something I wanted and I know that sounds terrible, but it's true. I really didn't. I don't think I even played with dolls when I was a girl. I was such a tomboy."

"And now look at you," said Charlie.

"If only you wore a suit to work. I'd be my fucking mother."

"I like your mother," said Charlie, feigning indignation.

"Me too," Claire said. "That doesn't mean I want to be her."

And it was on nights like these that Claire Apple, in the old farmhouse with her husband and her child, reached an accommodation with herself, something approaching peace. Nights when the cold outdoors did not matter for inside there was the steady pulsing of the woodstove with its orange glow of heat. Nights when the world had shrunk to include only the three of them and they were a family and on nights like this she did not know what else you could ask for. You had each other and the wood heat and the old house and that was enough.

But there were times later, as Jonah moved from infant to toddler to child, that she watched Charlie leave in the morning, watched him start the truck in the driveway from the kitchen window, when she felt something close to loss, and worst of all she knew it was not something she could speak about. Charlie was smart enough not to come out and say it, but Claire knew that once Jonah came he expected her to stay at home. There was a part of him that was old-fashioned—that loved having her in the kitchen before they had a child. Now, with Jonah, he expected her place to be at home.

The truth was that she was jealous of her husband, of the restaurant, of the life he now led outside the home.

Secretly she longed for the days when she had cooked with

absolute abandon, when the food was what mattered and everything else came second. Claire missed the hot stove, all the
burners fired up, the pans warped from the heat, waiting for a fil-
let of fish or pigeon thighs to be seared. She missed the tedium of
the prep work, the endless making of stocks and mother sauces.
She missed dicing onions and garlic, breaking down birds. She
missed the ritual repeating of orders as they were called to her
from the wait staff. She missed all of it, but most of all she
missed the freedom, the sense of personal identity she associ-
ated with cooking at Charlotte's. She missed being herself.

Sometimes Claire wanted to confess all of this to Charlie and
she thought she should. But she seemed to stop herself. What
kind of lousy mother wants to cook more than she wants to spend
time with her beautiful boy, a perfect child who thinks that she
defines the world.

In the mornings she watched Charlie leave and in the evenings she welcomed him home. In between she took care of
Jonah and sometimes she visited Charlotte's, which only made it
harder for her. And the seasons came and went. The years slid
by like low-flying clouds. And Claire Apple never said to her
husband what it was she felt, what it was she truly wanted. She
never told him about the emptiness that grew somewhere within
her, perhaps where the baby once was. She never told him how it
spread until it was how she thought of herself. She never told
him that sometimes in the middle of the day she dreamed of her
life going in different directions, she dreamed of her own place,
her own restaurant, of a life without a husband and a family. She
dreamed of other men: imagined them when she took long baths,
saw them running their hands over her body. Other men who
made love to her with the abandonment of youth, not the pre-

dictable movements of marriage. Claire hated herself for thinking these things; for dreaming these dreams. She hated herself
for wanting to stand alone. For wanting her life back. For wanting
herself back. In her heart, she knew it was too much to ask. And
so she only asked it to herself, and only during those moments
when she was alone and it could eat at her in peace.

Book Two

23

He came down the dirt road, his longish hair tucked under a baseball cap, a duffel bag, the kind that hockey players use, on his back. His boots sent little cyclones of dirt into the air with each step he took. He wore jeans and a leather jacket over a T-shirt. It was early October. Indian summer weather and the day was warm, too warm for his jacket, but he did not stop to take it off. Peak foliage had passed, though the bright red of the maple leaves still leaned over the road. Without the bag he would have fitted in, another hunter casing a road where he might look to get his deer. With the bag, his look tipped over to that of a vagabond, and you would not have stopped to pick him up had he had his thumb out. At one point he took a break from his walking at a bend in the Dog River and he sat down on a large granite rock that looked as if it were left here for this purpose and he lighted a cigarette.

He looked into the woods and he smoked. Buying the cigarettes had been a test. Stopping at the general store in town, he was not surprised to see Mrs. Morse still working the counter. She filled his request for the Camel Straights and looked right through him, as if he had not come in here nearly every day when he was a boy, as if he had not bought penny candy here, not picked up milk and cream and bread for home.

Below him the river ran low, water swirling around the smooth stones that made up the bed. Beyond the river the mottled light in the forest cast strange shadows, a fallen-down beech tree, caught in the branches of an evergreen, for a moment looked like the roof of a small cabin before he was able to make out what it was. He stubbed his cigarette out on the ground and stood and began to walk again.

The dirt beneath his feet was the color of sand. The land felt solid to him and he walked with the slightly bowlegged gait of a man accustomed to life at sea. Seventeen years had passed as fast as a rainstorm and he was coming home.

24

Claire was in the dining room at Charlotte's, replacing the flowers in the vases on the tables, when she suddenly realized she could no longer hear the steady bouncing of the tennis ball that seven-year-old Jonah had been throwing relentlessly against the side of the building. She stopped and listened for him. Nothing. Maybe he'd run around back, she thought.

Claire went to the front door of the restaurant and opened it. She looked out and she did not see her son. Then, stepping onto the granite block that led to the walkway, she saw him in the small parking lot and a man she had never seen before was down on one knee talking to him. Panic rose inside her. Charlie was out at one of the farms and would not be back for an hour at least and she did not like the look of this man. His hair was long and his face weathered and he had a bag next to him that suggested transience to her.

"Can I help you?" Claire shouted, moving quickly toward the two of them. Jonah turned and looked at her.

"Mommy," he said, his voice calm, not displaying any distress.

The man rose up. He was tall and he looked at her. A broad smile came across his weathered face. She saw now that he was handsome, remarkably so, with bright green eyes and high cheekbones, a firm jaw, a straight nose.

He said, "I heard you were looking for a chef."

"No," Claire said. "I'm sorry, are you sure it was Charlotte's?"

Jonah came to her, her little curly-haired boy, and stood half behind her legs. Good, she thought, this is where you should be. She unconsciously ruffled his hair.

"Yes," the man said, "I'm pretty sure it was Charlotte's." He looked away now, as if pondering this. "That's what I was told."

Claire shook her head. "Again, I'm sorry. But we're not hiring."

"The place looks good, Claire."

"How do you know my name?" asked Claire, and he smiled and she placed him then, underneath the hair and the beard, she saw the boy she had fallen in love with when she was a teenager. "Owen," she said.

"You're the last person I expected to see here."

"Charlie and I are married."

"Well, that's something," Owen said. "That's got be the smallest town thing I've ever heard."

"He tried to reach you."

"Yeah, I've been out of touch."

Claire nodded. "It's good to see you."

"You wouldn't have a beer at the bar in there, would you?"

"Of course," Claire said. "Come in. Please."

She brought him into the dining room. She had the curious feeling of displacement, the way one feels when suddenly the home they have always known is no longer theirs. Outside, she could hear Jonah once again playing his game with the tennis ball, the steady *smack smack smack* of ball against the old wood of the door. She had long ago given up asking him not to play it here, for this was a restaurant and there was nothing for a boy to do.

"Do you have any preference on the beer?" she finally said.

"Nah," Owen said. "Whatever you got."

"I'll be right back," said Claire, and she went to the bar and reached under to the sliding fridge. She opened it and took out a bottle of Copper Ale and she brought it over to him. He is your husband's brother, she told herself. Your brother-in-law. Whatever history you had was a lifetime ago. She wished Charlie would come back, but she also wished there was some way she could warn him. She knew his affection for his brother: he often said the two of them were raised like twins, inseparable, with a bond that ran deeper than others could understand. At the same time, it had been years since he had mentioned Owen's name, and the postcards that once came with numbing regularity had stopped altogether. She knew that Charlie felt betrayed somehow by this, as if his brother blamed him for their father's death, for the decision that had left Charlie with Charlotte's.

"Thanks," he said, and when he looked across at her, she saw how intense his gaze was, stronger than Charlie's, whose icy blue eyes always seemed benign, searching. Owen, by contrast, had deep green eyes, and when he looked at her fully she needed to look away. She had forgotten this about him. She used to love when he looked at her but now he made her feel small, powerless, and for some reason she did not trust him. Everything about him unnerved her.

In just a few minutes, though, she heard Charlie's voice outside, talking to Jonah, and she said, "Here he is."

Owen stood up. "Let's surprise him," he said.

"You don't think he's going to be surprised already?"

"I know, but let's really surprise him."

Owen moved toward the door, and leaned against the wall, so that when it opened he would be behind it. He was only there for a second when the door swung open and Charlie stood on the threshold, looking at Claire where she sat at the table, an open bottle of beer at the place across from her.

"Hey," he said. "Jonah said something about—"

Claire tried to signal him with her eyes, looking over toward the now-open door. Charlie looked puzzled.

He said, "What?" And in that moment the door behind him moved back toward closed, and he turned, and for an instant Claire saw his body coil, as if preparing to fight, and then she saw the recognition run through him, his arms going slack, and he said, "Jesus."

"Hello, Charlie," said Owen.

"I don't fucking believe it."

"Believe it, I'm here."

"You look like shit."

"Thanks, is that any way to treat your kid brother after, what, seventeen, eighteen years?"

"You need a haircut for starters."

"Give me a hug," said Owen, and Charlie did, and as Claire watched the two tall men wrap their arms around each other, as she saw their obvious affection, their sense of loss regained was palpable, and in that moment Claire thought, It's going to be okay. It's going to be okay after all.

OWEN HAD never planned to return. When he left Eden he thought it was for good.

He had done things, seen things, his brother never would. He had watched a giant orange sun fall into the South Pacific from the deck of a boat. He had made love to strange women and, sometimes, prostitutes, in port cities. He had smoked hashish in Turkish cafés. He had slept on benches; had been in fights in foreign bars where he was lucky to escape with his life. He had stolen. Once, while out on a Portuguese fishing trawler, he woke from a deep sleep to hear a commotion on the deck, where he found a circle of grown men having sex with a large fish that they held down with their boots.

Owen had dealt with the boredom, the hard work that was life at sea. He had spent countless hours applying heavy white and dull gray paint to all parts of ships under an unforgiving sun. He had cooked for men who had no appreciation for food beyond the bare sustenance it provided. He had grown used to the unyielding horizon, the sameness of the broad ocean, water all around him, but all of it useless except as a means of travel, and for the fish they sometimes caught with the lines they used to troll off the back of the large container ships.

Like his father, he took up smoking and he grew to love it. He smoked, like all the men he knew on freighters, to mark time. He drank more than he should, and when he could find drugs, no matter what they were, he used these, too. At least until their hold on him began to scare him or when a captain got a sense of what he was up to. Getting caught sniffing heroin was enough to blackball a man from the service for a long time. Not to mention the dangers posed by a small kitchen. You did not want to be too high in a kitchen at sea. Fire was the enemy of all boats.

He had slept with many women but he had loved none of them. Perhaps he loved them at the time, when they lay in his arms in the tropical heat; he loved their smell, the differences in each of them; he loved when they first undressed and he saw them, their breasts and their nipples, the darkness or paleness of their skin. He loved their shyness and their boldness and he loved that they gave themselves to him even though they knew he had little to give them in return. Even though they knew that in a few days he would leave without ceremony, moving on to wherever the ocean—and the company—took him next. He lived for the sounds of their voices, speaking to him in Vietnamese or Spanish or French. In the mornings he loved sitting in a chair and smoking and watching them sleep. Times when he could take in all of them and revel in the fact that they meant nothing to him beyond the warmth of their bodies in the dark of night.

Sometimes, though, as his brother had, he became aware of his heart. There was one woman in the Canary Islands, ten years, or more, older than him, with dark skin and long black hair and cocoa-colored eyes. He spent two weeks with her without learning her name, and back at sea he ached for her in a way he had not for the others. Smoking under the ocean stars, he thought about her. And he thought, So this is what it is all about. But he knew that like the others he would never see her again. And in that lay a certain comfort.

Owen moved from boat to boat, from job to job. He kept to himself and tried to stay out of trouble. His last ship, *The Mildred,* an enormous container ship that ran from Rotterdam to Santiago to Miami and back to Rotterdam again, was considered an ace job in the fleet. The pay was good. The captain, Arlen Cooper, was an old salt and known to be fair and competent. Most of the crew had worked there forever, and when there was an opening for a cook, Owen leaped at it.

At first everything went fine. He fit in and it was like any other job he had had. Then after a couple of weeks at sea it became clear to Owen that the first mate, Little Danny, had it out for him.

Little Danny wasn't little. He had been on another ship where the captain was named Dan and the name stuck. He was around Owen's age, a shade over six feet, and heavyset. From the get-go, he rode Owen harder than he needed to. Owen was not some greenie on his first trip. He knew his way around.

After a month of this, Owen finally decided to approach the captain. It was an unusual thing to do but Coop, as he was called, was said to be a good man. They spoke on the bridge and the captain heard him out and said he would talk to Little Danny. Owen thought that would be the end of it.

The next morning, Owen woke to weight on his legs. He opened his eyes, and there was Little Danny, sitting on Owen's legs on his bunk.

"What the—" said Owen.

"You ever talk to Coop about me again, I'll personally see you never get on another ship again."

"Get off me," said Owen.

Little Danny stood up. "You got me?"

"I got you," Owen said.

But it didn't end there either. Once, Owen entered the kitchen early in the morning to prep breakfast and Little Danny was already there, going through the stores.

"What are you doing?" Owen said.

"Inspection."

"Not in my galley," said Owen. "No one comes in my galley without asking. That includes you."

"I think you're confused about chain of command, my friend."

"Out," said Owen, and this time Little Danny left.

Owen was used to certain men not liking him. It was the way he looked, he knew. He was not one who made male friends easily and did not seek them out. He kept to himself at sea and on land and only asked the same in return from his crewmates. Other men knew how women reacted to him and he figured this had a lot to do with it. Little Danny was different though. He was determined to see Owen gone and in the end it was something innocent that got him.

Owen collected knives. Small knives he bought at different ports. One afternoon he was sitting on the landing of the narrow staircase that led to the bridge. He had a butterfly knife and was flicking it back and forth, and each time he did, the blade opened and then closed again. It was more of a nervous habit than anything. Something to do when he wasn't smoking. At that moment Little Danny came up the stairs and he gave Owen that smirk that Owen hated and Owen flicked the knife at him from three or four feet away. The blade flashed open and then closed. Little Danny stopped.

"What kind of knife is that?"

"Butterfly."

Little Danny nodded and went by. That afternoon the captain called Owen and told him he was letting him go in Miami. Little Danny had filed a report about the knife Owen had threatened him with.

"Coop, that's bullshit," Owen said.

"He wrote a report, Owen. Knives are serious business. So is the chain of command. I got no choice. You're blackballed."

And so like that, after seventeen years at sea, Owen Bender was no longer in the Merchant Marines. He didn't know what to do with himself. He spent a few weeks in Florida bumming around beach towns. Then he began to make his way north. He figured he'd get to the Cape and stop but as he traveled he began to think about Eden. What the hell, he thought. For a short time. Surprise his brother. Regroup. Start over. Think of something to do next.

25

His first night back in Eden, Owen lingered around the kitchen at Charlotte's and watched Charlie cook and tried to stay out of the way. He would never admit it but he was exhilarated by watching his brother cook, how accomplished he had become, better than their father, while Owen's skills had eroded from years of cooking food for men at sea. Claire was home with the boy, as she was all week, joining Charlie on weekends. An accommodation they had reached. These two nights a sitter watched Jonah. It was busy enough that Owen did not have much chance to talk to Charlie and spent much of his night out on the back porch smoking cigarettes, looking at the black river running through the trees in the dark.

After Charlie closed down, they returned to the house on Signal Ridge, and Jonah was in bed now, and Claire cooked for the two of them, a simple dinner of panfried steaks, roasted potatoes, and a green salad. They drank a big-bodied Cabernet and Owen told them about life at sea.

"Once," he said, "we were coming into the port of Guayaquil, in Ecuador, and it was late at night, and the large stick ship I was on moved slowly down this wide river. I was on watch, with two other men this night, since this was an area known for pirating. As the ship moved through the narrows, pulled by a tug, they came from all sides. Four or five speedboats pulled up to the boat. It was dark. Quiet. Then the sound of the grappling hooks they used landing across the rails of the deck. One of the men I was with ran inside, while the other two of us, without thinking, rushed the rail. Below we could see them. They were on rope ladders, climbing quickly toward us. I had a flare gun and I fired it. The flares shot across the river and lit up everything. The trees on the shore, their boats, the men below. They stopped for a moment, looked up at us, and then they just kept coming. I fired another one and this time they didn't hesitate. By the time I turned to head inside, it was too late. The other man with me had already left. Three men scrambled over the railing, and when I went to swing at one of them, I was hit from behind. And that's all I remember."

"My God," said Claire. "What happened?"

"They knocked me out," Owen said, fingering his wineglass. "Hit me with some makeshift weapon. No one came out to help me. Apparently I lay there while they cut the locks off the containers and began throwing cartons of stuff down to the boats below."

"What were you carrying?"

"Watches. That's what they got. Boxes and boxes of Rolexes."

"They must have known," said Charlie.

"Oh, yeah," said Owen. "Someone would find out what was coming in. We got hit at most of the major ports at least once."

"So were you okay?" asked Claire.

"Yeah. I mean, I had a hell of a headache for about a week. And anytime after that, if the ship got hit, I locked myself in my room. Let them have whatever they want. I'm not getting hurt protecting another man's stuff."

Owen looked across the table at his brother and then at his pretty wife. He met her eyes, and he sensed her discomfort. She was the most surprising part of all of this. He figured Charlie would have found a wife. He was the kind of guy who needed to get married. Who needed the security blanket that came with it. But that he married Owen's teenage love was something else. And she was a chef to boot. He wondered if sometimes she thought she had settled.

After dinner, Owen helped clear the dishes, but since Claire insisted on finishing the cleaning, he retired outside and Charlie joined him. They stood on the porch and Owen smoked and the air was cool with fall and smelled of wet leaves.

"When did you pick those up?" Charlie asked, motioning to the cigarette his brother drew on.

"Occupational hazard," Owen said.

"They'll kill you."

"One can hope, right?" said Owen.

"I was never tempted. Thank God. After Dad."

"You have any grass?"

"Grass?"

"Yeah, you know, pot. Like we used to."

Charlie laughed. "Not in a long time. Not since you were around, really."

Owen looked at his taller brother, at his serious face, his receding hairline. "I bet there's still roaches in the barn. Remember how we used to just leave them out there? For a rainy day?"

"Yeah," said Charlie, "I do. But they wouldn't be any good now."

"Fuck it," said Owen. "Let's find out."

And with that, he stepped off the porch onto the grass and began to move toward the barn. He suspected his brother would follow him, and he was right. They walked across the lawn and the light from Charlie and Claire's room upstairs shot across the grass and illuminated their walk.

When they reached the barn, Owen opened the old doors and stepped into the darkness. He sensed Charlie at his back, and he stopped for a moment and let his eyes adjust to the lack of light. When they had, he said, "This place hasn't changed."

"I almost never come out here," said Charlie.

"No?" said Owen. "This used to be your favorite place."

"Things change," Charlie said.

"You better go first," said Owen.

Charlie stepped in front of him, and in the thin light that came through the large doors, Owen watched his brother move across the earthen floor to the ladder against the south-facing wall and he followed him. Charlie grabbed the ladder and began to climb and Owen followed on his heels. When he emerged into the loft, it was even darker, and he waited a minute until he could make out his brother's shape, and hear his footfalls, moving across the beams toward where he knew from memory the large hay doors were.

"It's like stepping back in time," Owen said.

"Just watch your step," said Charlie. "Some of these floor-boards are like paper."

Owen moved forward gingerly, one foot in front of the other, and he was following the beams and the wood was solid under-neath his feet. He could not see his brother in front of him, though in a moment he no longer heard his steps, and then the hay doors opened and the wan light from outside suddenly streamed into the loft and he could make out the shadowy shape of his brother next to the opening. He had about fifteen feet to go and he made it easily now, and when he reached the edge, he sat down next to his brother, and he let his legs hang over the edge. A cold breeze came in from the east but it did not bother him.

Owen reached out and put his arm around Charlie's neck. "How about this?" he said. "Now all we need is a joint."

"Check behind the door," said Charlie.

Owen reached to his right, and felt along the wall, toward where seventeen years ago they had put their unfinished roaches. His fingers hit grainy wood and he moved them up till he found the small shelf that was there, and then he felt the small nubs of old joints, mixed in with the cobwebs. He grabbed whatever was there and brought it back, held the small pile in his hands, and in the dim light he saw that there were a number of old dried ends of marijuana joints.

"Look at this," he said. "Just as I thought. Get stoned with me, Charlie."

"I can't," Charlie said. "But help yourself."

"Why not?"

"Not my thing anymore, that's all."

"Suit yourself," said Owen, and he began to unroll the old

joints, the mixture of ash and dried pot crumbling into his hands. "Most likely sucks anyway."

From the pack of cigarettes in his pocket he took one out and carefully took the paper away from the tobacco, letting it spill into the air below him. He took the mixture in his other palm and pressed it into the paper, rolling it slowly so that it would not rip. He licked it together and then shook it. "There," he said.

He put the jury-rigged joint to his lips and he lighted it, his face and then his brother's caught in its brightness before it extinguished and the joint was cherry red and he sucked on it. He inhaled deeply and then he coughed, for the old dry pot was harsh and hurt his lungs. But he felt its bite instantly, for though it was old, it still had what it took and it went to his head. He held it out for Charlie.

"You sure?" he said.

"Yeah," said Charlie, "I'm sure."

Owen took two more long drags on the joint and then it was so low it was at his fingers and he tossed it into the yard, watching its red tip spin in the air before landing on the grass below them. The wind picked up then, and they could hear the weather vane on the roof as it spun on its rusty axis. To their left was the old house, and the kitchen light had gone off since they had gotten up here, and the only light came from the upstairs bedroom, around the corner from the barn, so that Owen could not see into it. They sat in silence for a while, as they had as youths.

Charlie broke the silence. He said, "Don't take this the wrong way. But can I ask you your plan?"

"Let me see," said Owen. "I don't really have one."

"You can stay as long as you want, you know that."

"Thanks," Owen said. "Don't worry about it. I won't mess up your perfect life here."

"I'm not worried about that, I was just wondering if you were going back. Back to the Merchant Marines."

Owen sighed. "I don't think so."

Charlie did not ask. "Okay," he said.

"Can I get back to you?"

"Of course, I was just curious. You can have the downstairs room tonight and for as long as you need it."

Owen nodded. "I appreciate that."

Charlie went to speak and then paused. "You could—"

"What?"

"Nothing. I was just going to say you could come work at Charlotte's again while you figure out your next move."

"Let me think about that one."

"All right," said Charlie. "And now I need to get to bed. Tomorrow morning is going to come fast enough as it is."

"Before you go," Owen said.

"Yes?"

"Congratulations."

"Congratulations?"

"On all of this. And Claire."

"I was worried you might be, you know."

"It was a long time ago."

"Yeah," said Charlie.

They stood then, and walked back the way they had come. When they reached the porch, Owen stopped. "I'm going to stay out for one more smoke."

They said good night, and Owen watched as his brother opened the old screen door and disappeared into the house.

Owen took his cigarettes out of his breast pocket and he took one out and he lighted it. He left the porch for the yard and he looked up into the black sky, the stars brighter now than they were earlier, the thin moon fully risen, almost directly above. He looked across the field, past the barn, to the black woods where a lifetime ago his father had taken his own life. Many times out on the ocean he thought about that day. He had thought about the two of them running through the woods in the heavy rain, knowing what was in front of them, but having no choice but to continue on. Sometimes he wondered if he could ever go into those woods again, if he could ever move through the forest with the innocence of childhood, and he decided that he could not.

Owen turned back to the house. The light in his brother's bedroom was still on. He saw his shirtless brother move past the window, and a moment later he saw Claire as well, and she stopped for a moment in front of it, as if looking out to him. She wore what appeared to be a white nightgown, and her arms were bare. He stared up at her. He drew on his cigarette, knowing that it would attract attention to his face. Claire moved away from the window. Owen smiled to himself. The lights in their room went out, and he was left alone, standing on the hard earth in the dark, the wind picking up again. He tossed his cigarette out into the field, watched it tumble through the air until it vanished into the high grass.

26

After a week at the old farmhouse, Owen sank his mea-
ger savings into the purchase of an old Silver Stream
trailer on three acres of hilly woods on the Hunger
Mountain Road. The land was rugged, thick and dense with high
spruce and rocky forest floor, but it was high enough to have a
sliver of view to the mountains to the west, and the sun fought
through this gap and threw streams of afternoon light onto the
small trailer. Inside was a potbellied woodstove, a small kitchenette with a two-burner cookstove and a tiny refrigerator, a narrow living room with a built-in sofa, one rocking chair, and a
place for a television. A curtain divided the small platform bed
from the rest of the living area.

It was a class-four road, little more than a cow path and not maintained by the town, and he had enough money left over to buy himself an old Toyota truck, one of those classic Vermont vehicles where the bed had been replaced by a wooden one. But he could lock the tires and have four-wheel drive and this was essential to climb the road in winter and in mud season.

His last night at the house was a Sunday and the restaurant was closed, and Owen cooked for Claire and Charlie as a thank-you for putting him up in the house he had grown up in but that now belonged only to them. It had been a long time since he had done anything ambitious but somehow from the depths of his memory he summoned his father's coq au vin. He served it, as his father had done, over buttered egg noodles and with lightly fried asparagus bundles.

Outside the night was dark and cool and they ate in the dining room and from the living room they could hear the woodstove as it ticked with the heat of new wood. Jonah had been sent to bed and it was just the three of them. As they ate, they talked in general terms about Charlotte's, about Owen's new place in the woods. Claire and Charlie were careful not to be condescending about his trailer, though both of them wondered how he could live there, in space that small, on land that dark and unforgiving. But what they did not know was that to Owen it offered, if less light, then greater space than he had grown used to on the tight quarters of a boat. And, for the first time in his life, something besides the clothes on his back would be his and his alone.

When dinner was finished, Charlie brought up the idea of Owen working at Charlotte's. Owen knew it was a pro forma gesture, that in truth neither Charlie nor, especially, Claire wanted him there but that they had to offer. And for a moment, the possibility of accepting intrigued him, if only for this reason. And as he looked across the table at Claire, at her big wet eyes, he wanted to say yes, if only to see her discomfort increase.

Owen said, "That's nice of you, Charlie, it really is. But you know it's not my bag. I've been making bad food for twenty years, why stop now?"

Charlie crossed his hands on the table in front of him. "I think it would be nice. And I can use the help. Claire can only be there on weekends now."

Owen nodded at Claire. "What do you think, Claire? A few too many Benders in the kitchen?"

Claire smiled shyly and looked away. Owen knew she had trouble making eye contact with him and this did not surprise him for he knew that a lot of women did. For the same reasons women were drawn to him they were also frightened of him, of the strength of his gaze.

Claire said, "We could use the help. That's true. Charlie's been doing the work of two, maybe three, really, for a long time now. Maybe he would even get a night off and we could do something as a family."

Owen watched as she reached out and placed her hand over her husband's own. It was a subtle and natural movement, one that wives the world over do. But in its subtlety he saw something else, too. A reminder of how different things were between him and his brother, that seventeen years had passed and there was no going back.

Owen slowly stood from the table, making his way outside for a cigarette. He stopped and put a hand on his brother's shoulder, shot a long look at Claire. "I appreciate it, I do," he said. "But I'll be all right. I will."

———

OWEN TOOK a job cooking at Camel's, a dive bar on the outside of town. It was a low-ceilinged place with a wooden bar warped from age and scratched up from generations of patrons carving their initials and other things into it. It had a pool table and the light was dim and sometimes on Friday and Saturday nights there was live music and people danced. The food was nothing special, burgers and fries and the occasional salad, but it was work he was used to, not much different from cooking for men at sea, with the obvious and important difference that it was a bar that employed young barmaids and there was something, Owen thought, to be said for this.

On nights when the kitchen grew quiet, Owen sat at the old bar and nursed bourbons and smoked his cigarettes.

Sometimes he chatted with the women who worked there. They were local girls mostly, girls who wore blue eye shadow and were killing time until they married someone they had known since elementary school.

He knew they were all curious about him. Where he had been, what he had done, what his story was. He knew they liked his longish blond hair, his weathered, handsome face, his green eyes, his tall, lean body, the way he carried himself, which spoke of stories from other places even though he, like them, had spent his childhood among these gentle hills. He knew they whispered about him, imagined fucking him, talked about it the way women always had near him, and sometimes, generally more out of boredom than desire, he brought one of them home with him.

In the half dark he would undress her, lay her down on his

narrow bed, and move his hands over her. Bring her, slowly and deliberately, to places boys her own age could not. Knowing where she liked to be touched, how to be slow and patient.

He made love to them in ways he knew they wanted to be made love to and he did so not out of some great sense of self-lessness or passion for the particular woman, but rather because he understood what it was they ached for and he knew that there were few things in this life that came easily to him and this was one of them. He also liked their gratitude, left unspoken but something he could feel when they were finished and lay to-gether, sweaty and intertwined, falling apart naturally, like objects caught in a vacuum after it lifts.

In the mornings Owen would wake and for a brief moment forget they were there, rolling over to find some woman half his age sprawled out on the other side of his bed, her makeup wanting to run off her face, her nakedness not nearly as interesting to him as it had been in the drunken dark of the night before. He would take in the whole of her: the pertness of her young breasts, the place where her thighs came together; how her body moved with the collective hum of sleep.

And then he would leave before they stirred, getting into his truck on mornings when he could see his breath, letting them find their own way to whatever corner of Eden they happened to call home. No promises, no commitments, nothing more than a warm body to mute the chill of the season.

27

Right before Thanksgiving it snowed for ten days in a row, a heavy, wet snow that clung to the spruce trees and piled high against the sides of the buildings in Eden. It fell with the intensity of rain. Snow that made the roads tricky; that felled trees with its weight and knocked out the electric grid for entire days, sparing businesses like Charlotte's that knew enough to have generators for backup.

By Thanksgiving Day it had stopped and the sunlight was almost blinding as it reflected off the meadows that Owen drove by on his way to the house on Hunger Mountain. Charlie had come by Owen's trailer the day before, on a morning when the wind blew heavy drifts on the sides of the road. Owen did not have a phone, so Charlie had driven out to invite him over. They had stood together in the driveway, Owen in only a flannel shirt and jeans, and the falling flakes had clung to their hair.

"Turkey and all the fixings," Owen said. "How American of you."

"It's just dinner," Charlie said. "Get you out of the bar for a day."

Owen smiled. "What makes you think I want out of the bar?"

"You know what I mean."

"All right," he said, "you got me. What time?"

"There's one other thing," said Charlie. "Mom is going to be there."

"I think I'll just hang here," said Owen.

"Come on, Owen, it's not that big a deal."

Owen brushed snow off his eyebrows. "I thought she never comes back here."

"She doesn't. She came for my wedding. And now she's coming to see you."

"That's too much for me, man. I'm just getting used to being back here. Getting my legs still."

"She wants to see you."

"Yeah, well."

"Listen," said Charlie. "One day. That's all. Is that too much to ask? That for one day we try to be a family?"

Owen looked across at his big brother. At the earnestness coming from his blue eyes. He shook his head and laughed. "Fuck," he said. "Fucking holidays. That was a good thing about being at sea, you know? We'd defrost the best steaks and get drunk and call it Christmas. Out in the middle of nowhere, somewhere near the equator. No bullshit. No drama."

"There won't be any drama," said Charlie.

"Sounds like I don't have a choice."

"You don't."

Now, driving to the farmhouse, Owen smoked cigarettes and thought about Charlotte, about his father, about Charlie, about how everything turned out.

HIS MOTHER had aged well. She was the first one he saw when he came through the door and she smiled at him, crow's-feet emanating out from her beautiful green eyes, the eyes he'd inherited. She wore a long black skirt, a red shirt, a black cardigan. She looked very hip for her age, very New York. She was the timeless beauty she had always been. Charlotte.

She held her arms out wide and he thought, If she does not cry then I will. But as his mother came to him, as he took her into his arms, doing what he did not want to do but what came naturally, he felt her hands running through his long hair.

"Owen," she said, and in her voice he heard the tears before he saw them.

"Don't, Mom," he said.

"You smell like cigarettes."

Owen held his mother away from him. "That's funny," he said. "I just smoked a cigarette."

"I'm still your mother," she said.

"I know."

"I can say things."

"Say anything you want."

Owen looked at her, her blond hair now elegantly streaked with gray, his mother. He looked at her for signs of strain, to see if being back in this house redolent with memories was having any effect on her. But he knew her strength, the sense of propriety she had instilled in all of them: the stoic widow, never showing the world her pain.

"I need a drink," Owen said.

"There is stuff in the dining room," his mother said.

"I'll find it," said Owen, and he left her in the foyer of the old house.

In the dining room the table was set for the four adults and for young Jonah, who was nowhere to be seen. From here Owen could see through to the kitchen, and he caught a glimpse of Claire kneeling in front of the oven, her hair tied back, and she did not see him and for a moment he watched her. Watched her look in on what he figured was the obligatory bird. She stared into the open oven, brushed a lone bang of hair away from her face. Then she closed the oven and stood and suddenly, as if aware of his gaze, she turned to see him there in the dining room and she smiled at him. Her black eyes flashed.

"Hi, Owen," she said.

Owen lifted the bottle of bourbon off the table as a return greeting. He smiled. She moved out of his sight, into the kitchen. He poured a stiff three fingers of the bourbon into a tumbler and drank it right down. Filled it again and drank this in two swallows. Filled it a third time and moved into the kitchen. Toward the one day of family he had promised his brother.

THEY ATE a meal their father would have been proud of. Fat Prince Edward Island oysters on the half shell with a mignonette sauce. A roast wild turkey stuffed with chestnuts, black truffles, walnuts, and rice. An au jus gravy. Leeks braised in white wine and cream. Sweet potatoes whipped with maple syrup, vanilla bean, and butter. An apple pie made from local McIntosh apples and served with a coffee ice cream Charlie had made that morning.

They ate in the dining room and outside the sun was setting early, the sky a mottle of reds and blues. They all sat around the table, even little dark-haired Jonah, who reminded Owen of himself and Charlie at that age, polite and quiet, used to the ritual of dinner, a child of the restaurant. The alcohol was helping Owen. The bourbons before dinner and now the parade of wines with it allowed him to forget his misgivings. It allowed him to block out the history that this house, this life, this life that had once belonged to his father but had since been swallowed by his brother and by the comely Claire, did not normally let him bury the way he thought he must if he was to survive. Was that what it was all about? Survival? Learning to let things behind you *be* behind you? Embrace the present, live in the moment, and all that other bullshit. That was what Owen said to himself when he was sober. For now, it was less relevant. He was drunk. And he was managing to enjoy himself. Telling stories and listening to Charlie and Claire and Charlotte. Watching his nephew, his arms out from his body, spinning like an airplane in the kitchen after dinner.

AFTER DINNER, Owen moved to the porch to smoke. It was dusk now and in front of him was the snow-covered field and beyond it the spruce trees at the start of the forest rose like sentinels.

There was little moon. There was the noise from the kitchen where the dinner dishes were being washed and there was the sound of his lighter as he lit his cigarette and there was nothing else, only the steady sound of his breathing as he smoked and the early winter wind that twisted and turned the creaky, rusty weather vane on the roof of the barn to his right. Despite all the snow it was not cold. Or maybe it was the booze. He was immune to the cold when he was drunk.

He finished one cigarette and lit another. Above him a light went on upstairs and sent light out onto the snow and he knew from his brief time living here that this was Claire putting Jonah to bed.

Behind him the door opened and he half turned, expecting to see Charlie, but instead it was his mother. She gave an exaggerated shiver and pulled her sweater closer around her. She moved and stood next to him.

"I don't know how you stand the cold," she said.

"I don't think about it."

"You remind me of Charles right now."

"It's the smoking."

"Yes," said Charlotte. "There's that. Standing on the porch, smoking in the cold. That was your father all right. But it's more the way you look. The way you are staring into the woods. Searching."

Owen smiled at her. Dragged on his cigarette. "I wouldn't read that much into it," he said. "I'm just not that deep."

"Oh, I think you are," said Charlotte. "Deeper than you even know. You were always more soulful than your brother. And I don't mean that as an insult to Charlie. You just were. Love and life come easier for him, that's all. He isn't as verbal as you, so I

think that is sometimes mistaken for introspection. But you wonder and think about things. You have a harder time forgiving.
Forgetting. We all do, of course. But sometimes, too, we need to
let go."

Owen field-stripped his cigarette, sending the tip out into the
yard, putting the spent filter back into the pack he kept in his
breast pocket. "Sounds like the wine talking, Charlotte," he
said. "Trust me, I'm fine."

"All I'm saying," said Charlotte, "is that you can't fool your
mother."

Owen turned to his mother. "Give me a hug," he said. "I'm
going home."

Charlotte came to him and he took her in his arms and hugged
her briefly, and when they separated he saw that her eyes were
moist and he wanted to say something but there was nothing.

THAT NIGHT, after Owen returned home, he sat for a while on the
front steps of the trailer and he looked out to the gap in the trees
where he could see the stars, bright and close in the near-winter
night. Though his head was swimming from the food and drink,
he nursed a final bourbon and smoked his cigarettes and
watched the night sky.

It was cold but the density of the trees kept out the wind that
rustled the branches high above. When he looked away he remembered his father's words: "Don't think too much on what you
can never understand. Focus instead on the small mysteries.
What we can know. What we can hold in our hands. This is all
that counts."

And as he thought this, he turned his attention to the day now past, to his mother, and to Charlie, to the old house on Signal Ridge that they collectively pretended held no significance. A house that did not hide the truth of the past, as if it were any other house on any other hill in Eden, his brother's residence and nothing more. Not the place of his childhood. Not the place where in the woods on a rainy afternoon his father had blown his head off with a single shot from a deer rifle.

He took a long pull of his bourbon and he suddenly pictured Claire. Saw her in front of the oven as he had seen her earlier that day, kneeling down to check on the progress of the roast. Saw her brush the hair out of her eyes, saw the shape of her through her clothes, and he remembered making love to her many years before, in his bedroom when no one was home, at her parents' house when they were away, up at the lake on summer nights when they sneaked out. That was when Eden was perfect. They were young and thought they knew love and it seemed nothing could stop them. He remembered how strong he felt then. How nothing worried him. How all you needed was a girl, the summer, a little change in your pocket. Nothing was complicated. Now he had seen too much, been too many places. He had tasted too many things, lived longer and harder than a man of his years should. He had stopped believing.

And the truth was that while he could return to Eden, on some vital level Eden could never return to him.

28

That winter the two brothers reached an unspoken accord around how they would share the small town of their birth. It should not have been difficult. Charlie was perfectly willing to let the years wash away, to return to how, in his mind, things should have evolved all along. He had no concerns about sharing the restaurant, as long as the years he had spent shaping Charlotte's into his own image were taken into account. He had no concerns about sharing his life with Owen, about bringing him closer to his family, to his work. In fact, when Owen first returned, Charlie thought that this was how it would happen. He figured Owen would become the friend he had never had all these years he'd been married both to his wife and to the business. He saw the two of them getting right back into it, as they had as children, playing and hunting and fishing and, yes, cooking, together. It never occurred to him that there was another way, and the only thing he worried about was how Claire would adapt to having his younger brother around. There were two of them and then there were three, and now he was asking her to allow room for a fourth. And a fourth she had a history with.

Still, even after it became clear that Owen intended to strike out on his own and build his own life in Eden, Charlie found himself trying hard to reach out, to understand his brother, to fulfill the promise of the lifetime friendship they had seemed destined for until it was all blown up so many years ago.

On Sundays, nights when none of them had to work, Charlie insisted that Owen come to dinner, and mostly he did. Some nights he simply did not show, and since he did not have a phone, Charlie had no way of knowing until he arrived whether or not he would be there. But more often than not he showed and the three of them ate a late dinner after Jonah was in bed and they drank wine and they talked.

Sometimes Owen would stay late and they would sit in front of the woodstove and nurse Scotches, and on these nights whatever tension existed between them went away and they would wander back to earlier times, to silly stories about school as kids, about growing up in the restaurant, about their parents and their parents' friends, the drunken parties that in the early days of Eden filled the lawn behind the house they sat in. And in the telling of them the two brothers grew closer together and this pleased Charlie. If Claire felt excluded from this bonding she did not express it. Instead she asked questions to keep a story going and she'd laugh when they did, the three of them shaking their heads with the shared knowledge family intimacy brings.

One beautiful January morning, Owen appeared in the kitchen window while Claire and Charlie were having coffee and he held up a pair of snowshoes at his brother. Charlie smiled and looked at his wife.

"What are you waiting for?" she said. "Go ahead."

Charlie suited up and joined his brother out on the snowy pasture. The sky was cloudless, the sun bright and high. Though it was cold the air was invigorating and their breath showed when they spoke. The snow in front of them sparkled like a field of crystals.

They set out toward the forest, not downhill toward where they had found their father, but uphill, behind the house, heading across what was once the apple orchard toward the high woods. The snowshoes moved effortlessly across the field of white, and they used cross-country ski poles for balance.

Owen led and Charlie followed and they did not speak and the only sound was the steady crunch of the snow under the large aluminum snowshoes. Soon they had reached the woods' edge and the house was below them now, and they stopped for a moment before they hiked into the trees and watched the smoke spilling out of the chimney of the old farmhouse, the bright sky and the frosty mountains beyond it.

"Ready?" said Owen.

"You're the one with the pack-a-day habit," Charlie said.

Owen laughed. "Just for that, we're going all the way to Blue Pond."

They entered the forest now, and it was mostly white birch and beech here, trees that dated from the turn of the century, trees that were surprisingly tall and slender given their age. In front of them was the closest thing to a path, not a deer run exactly but a place where the trees formed a natural canopy. The snow below them was unmarked by animals. It was a steady pitch upward and they went quickly, Charlie marveling at his brother's strength, strength that did not seem possible given how Owen spent his nights, how he treated his body.

They climbed steadily and soon they were among groves of dense spruce and hemlock, darker in here, and they picked up a deer run, the path worn with tracks, pebbly pockets of shit here and there on either side, bark missing from the trees from the spring rut. The land flattened and the run was wide enough that they were able to walk side by side.

"When's the last time you were up here?" Owen said.

"Forever," said Charlie.

"Me too. I used to come up here to drink beer in high school."

"I remember. You had so many friends. And girls. I was always Owen's brother. 'Aren't you Owen's brother?' Didn't seem fair."

"Well, it comes around," Owen said, leaning back for a moment as the trail began to climb again. "Now I'm Charlie's brother."

"I don't know about that," Charlie said.

"Charlie's no-good brother," Owen said.

"No one thinks that," Charlie said quickly.

"Except for Claire."

Charlie stopped, breathing hard from the exertion. He leaned on one of his poles, looked at his brother, his brother with the long hair, the scraggly beard, the jawline he envied. "What do you mean by that?"

Owen started to walk again, lifting each leg high, placing the large shoe down on the deep snow beneath. "She doesn't like me," he said.

"That's not true," said Charlie, catching up. "What makes you think that?"

"I can tell. I know women."

"Well, I know Claire and she's never said anything like that to me."

"It's not always what they say. It's what they do. What they show you with their eyes, their body language. She doesn't like me. I can tell."

"I think she's probably just not used to having you around. You guys were high-school sweethearts, for Christ's sake. It's weird for her. That's all."

"And I never called her."

"When?"

"All those years ago," said Owen. "How about Blue Pond?" he then said, changing the subject.

"I'm not sure you're up to it."

"Catch me," Owen said.

THEY MADE good time over the top of Signal Ridge. The winter light fought through the heavy evergreens and in front of them there were small clearings where the sun shone brightly off the white of the pack.

Soon they had crested the large hill and they stopped. In front of them were piney woods and the land swooped down away from them, and though they could not see it, they knew that it rose again to the next ridge, and beyond that, another ridge. This land was a series of high ridges, mountain foothills leading to the west.

From the pocket of his coat Owen took out a metal flask and unscrewed the top. He put it to his lips and sipped from it.

"What kind of rotgut are you drinking now?" said Charlie.

"Bourbon," Owen said, and handed the flask to his brother.

"A little won't hurt," Charlie said, and drank from it. It was sharp and sweet and warm and it puckered his lips. He took another pull and handed it back.

Owen drank from it and then he lit a cigarette. The smoke spilled out of his mouth and nose and into the thin air.

"When you going to give them up?" said Charlie.

"As soon as you stop asking me," Owen said.

"Well, if you're going to smoke, then I'm going to beat you to the pond," Charlie said, and he began to walk again.

The escarpment was steep and he felt it in his legs, muscles he did not use every day. The tree cover was heavier as he went down and the air was suddenly cold and there was less light. In places the going was tricky, snow mixed with ice underfoot, and Charlie had to fix the claw of each shoe before moving forward.

When he reached the bottom, he turned and looked behind him. No sign of Owen. Charlie smiled to himself and he began the ascent over the next ridge, the one that led to Blue Pond.

By the time he reached the top, he was out of breath and he stopped for a moment and stuck his poles into the snow and rested his gloved hands on his knees. When the wind came back to him, he looked down and he could see the pond now, not blue at all but white and ice-covered. It was beautiful nonetheless, the forest walls moving up and away from it, a small hidden mountain lake. It had been a long time since he had been to it and he could never hike here without thinking of his father, who had taken them to the pond one summer morning when they were still young boys, forcing them along on the difficult walk. When they reached the shore, he told them that the lake contained a giant prehistoric fish, capable of eating children. Charlie remembered staring at the black water, wondering if it was lurking there, staring back up at them, waiting to rise from the depths. It was not until he was in his teens that he realized the story was nonsense, a story fathers told children to scare them away from swimming on their own.

The memory of this energized Charlie, and he grabbed his poles and began to hike down the hill. The trees thinned out and the sun was bright and he made good time. He looked back to see if he could see his brother but he could not. About halfway down the ridge, he was below the lake and he lost sight of it. He went quickly, one shoe in front of the other, using the poles to propel him along. He had a second wind and soon he was at the bottom and all that lay between him and Blue Pond was a small hillock dense with evergreens.

He charged up it, the path narrowing considerably through the trees, and as he hiked he listened again for Owen but his was the only sound in the woods. So much for beating me here, Charlie thought.

Finally he rounded the bend that led to the lake and there it was, the flat expanse of snow-covered water, a lake of resounding beauty in the summer months, stark and bare in the winter, the bottom of a bowl.

When he reached where the trees ended and the broad rocky shoreline began, he was so fixated on what was in front of him, the lake and the forest walls rising up on the opposite shore, that he heard his brother before he saw him. He turned to his left and in front of him was Owen, sitting on a rock as if he had been there for a while, smoking a cigarette, the flask of whiskey propped on his thigh, leaning against his jacket. It was his laughter Charlie had heard, a low, throaty chuckle.

"You made it," Owen said.

Charlie just stood there looking at him. He shook his head. "What, did you fly here?"

"I went around," said Owen. "It's a lot steeper but if you move it, it's faster."

Charlie went to his brother, sat next to him. He pointed at the whiskey. "Give me that."

Owen handed him the flask and Charlie sipped long and hard from it. He looked at Owen and smiled. "I got to hand it to you," he said. "I thought I'd left you in the dust."

"And not for the first time," said Owen.

29

That night at Charlotte's, Charlie could already feel the soreness that the morning would bring. But he felt awake and alive from the vigorous exercise. It was a slow night for Charlotte's, and he turned out a basic menu for the restaurant. A rack of lamb with a marjoram wine sauce was the big seller.

Back at the house, Claire had made a polenta with pancetta and Parmesan and it was hearty and warm and they ate in front of the woodstove with a rich red wine and watched the fire as it glowed behind the glass. Charlie normally stayed up after she went to bed, trying to wind down from the night of cooking, but tonight he followed her to bed and for the first time in a long time he rolled into her, and lit only by the full winter moon, they made love.

Charlie did not know why their lovemaking had become occasional at best. They did not talk about it. Sometimes he chalked it up to their schedules, to having a child, but he knew it was more than that. They had grown stale with each other and he did not know how to breathe life into their sex. He was still attracted to her. Some mornings he'd watch her walking around the bedroom in her nightgown and the sight of her stirred him.

Tonight, though, it was as if they were who they were many years ago, when she first came to the restaurant and he wanted nothing more than to linger together, to slow things down, to just be.

Charlie climbed on top of her and she said "I love the weight of you" and he looked down at her dark eyes, the slight roundness of her mouth as it opened when he pushed into her, and with his hands he reached underneath her and pulled her as far onto him as he could. Claire stretched her arms above her head and with one hand Charlie held both of hers together.

They came apart. Lay together looking at the ceiling. Outside the window Charlie could see the smoke from the chimney caught in the moonlight as it drifted up and out over the valley. He could see the bright full moon, all alone in the black sky. He could hear Claire's steady breathing next to him.

Charlie turned and looked at his wife. She was awake, clearly so, and as he turned she turned, too, and caught his eyes with her own. He said, "Owen thinks you don't like him."

"He said that?"

From her tone Charlie sensed that he had made a mistake. He

plugged on anyway. "Pretty much. I don't want to put words in his mouth. But he worries about it."

Claire sighed and as she did her breasts rose beneath the comforter. "That's bullshit," she said.

"I know."

"You do?"

"Yeah."

Claire looked toward the window, toward the night. "It's strange for me, that's all. I mean, I knew what I was getting into when we got married. Owen and I—that was a long time ago. But still. Sometimes I just feel uncomfortable around him. I wish it wasn't that way but it is. He's your brother. That gives him a place in our lives that I cannot control."

"We need to get past that," said Charlie.

"I'll talk to him."

"No, don't. Really. I shouldn't have brought it up. I shouldn't have. I really shouldn't have. It was a mistake."

Claire stared at him and then her eyes looked away, toward the foot of the bed. "I will. I'll talk to him. Don't worry, I'll be nice. You know how I am. I don't believe in tiptoeing around things. I say what I think. But I'll do it at a time when it's right. He's my brother-in-law. That means something."

Through the darkness Charlie nodded. "I wish you wouldn't."

"That isn't good enough," said Claire.

"Let's go to sleep," he said.

And after he said it, he slid down next to her and he hugged her, his face nuzzling against her neck. Claire put her arms around his neck and they stayed this way until he rolled away.

30

In the morning, Claire stood in the cold, clear air at the end of the long driveway and waited for the yellow school bus to makes its way down the hill and pick up Jonah. It was a ritual they shared every morning when it was not summer. They stood and looked up the hill and held hands and they could see their breath in the air. Then the bus would round the corner and she'd pick her son up in her arms, give him a kiss, knowing that soon the time would come when she would embarrass him, as her parents had embarrassed her, but that for now he was young enough to take her affection, to genuinely miss her when he walked up those steps, turning around for a moment before vanishing into the depths of the bus.

When the bus pulled away she waited until she could not see

it anymore, and then she began the slow, long walk up the driveway to the house. Inside, she warmed herself in front of the stove
before she set to making Charlie his breakfast. It was some of the
only cooking she did now during the week and the simplicity of
it pleased her. Of seeing eggs sunny-side up, of listening to the
toaster click with the sound of bread that was done. Of smelling
the local bacon as it snapped in the pan. The whole kitchen full
of smells and sounds while her husband still slept upstairs.

When everything was done, she climbed the staircase and
wandered into their bedroom and woke Charlie. He was a good
sleeper and he always came to slowly, and when he rubbed his
eyes, she told him breakfast was ready. That it was time to go.

By the time he came downstairs, freshly showered, Claire was
ready with his mug of strong black coffee, and she sat him down
and they ate with the silence of morning and it was the life of a
housewife, a life she had never wanted, but one that on week-
days she resigned herself to. Soon he would put on his coat and
she would watch his truck leave the driveway, the exhaust gray
in the cold and spilling into the air as he went. She would wait
until he was gone. She would let him go where she wanted to be,
to Charlotte's, to the work that she, too, loved.

ONCE HE was gone, Claire took a shower. The water was hot and
she stayed under it for a time. Afterward, she dressed, putting on
a black turtleneck and jeans, and downstairs she put on her winter boots and her coat.

Outside she climbed into her car and began to drive, down Signal Ridge, and then picked up the Old County Road. She passed

cars and trucks as she drove on the dirt roads and the drivers all waved, the way people did in Eden, and she waved back.

She was on her way to Owen's, and though she had never been there, she knew where it was. The Hunger Mountain Road was a road that she used to drive with Owen when they were in high school, on summer nights when the air was warm and they rode with the windows down and followed the curve of the earth up and over the eastern side of the mountain. It figured, Claire thought, that he would end up there now.

By the time she pulled into Owen's driveway—seeing for the first time the Silver Stream trailer, looking small and buried in high snow—it was almost eleven. She had no idea what his schedule was, though his truck was here, next to several cords of stacked wood protected by a large blue tarpaulin. She pulled in behind it. Got out of the car. She suddenly got a sense of altitude, of space beyond the trees, and when she looked she realized she could see halfway across Eden, to other mountains in the distance. Somewhere below her was Charlotte's, she thought to her west but she did not have her bearings. Claire took a deep breath and went to the door.

She knocked lightly and listened. Nothing. She knocked again, a little more assertively this time, and was about to knock again when it opened. In front of her stood Owen, wearing only a pair of jeans, shirtless and without shoes. He moved his shaggy hair out of his face. Claire looked away.

"I woke you," she said.

"Don't be silly. I needed to get up anyway. Come in."

Owen stepped away from the door and Claire climbed up into the trailer, and it was dark and it took a moment for her eyes to adjust. On her left was the woodstove and on the right a small kitchenette. Beyond it was a living room and then his bed. It smelled of wood smoke and cigarettes, the ripeness of old beer.

"You can put your coat on the chair," Owen said.

"Thanks," said Claire. She took off her coat and slung it over one of the chairs that surrounded a card table.

"You want some coffee? Tea?"

"Are you having any?"

"Coffee," he said.

"Sure."

"Have a seat," he said.

Claire pulled out one of the chairs and sat down. Owen still had not put a shirt on and while he made coffee Claire could not help but watch him. He was tall and his long torso was wiry and lean. Beautiful as he had always been, only less boyish now. He had filled out some.

Owen ground coffee beans and the sound filled the small trailer. Claire watched as he boiled water, and poured from the kettle through a sieve into a stainless-steel container. He filled two mugs and brought them over to the table.

"I hope black is okay," he said. "I don't keep any milk or cream in the house."

"Black is fine," said Claire.

Owen sat down across from her. He sat with his legs slightly open and he still wore no shirt and for the first time she noticed his tattoo: it was on his chest above his right nipple, a small black umbrella.

"I like your tattoo," she said.

Owen looked down. "Oh, yeah. You know, in case it rains."

Claire laughed in spite of herself. A nervous laugh. He made her nervous. Uncomfortable. As if she were not a woman of her age, as if she were not fully in control. "How long have you had it?"

Owen shrugged. "I don't know. Ten, fifteen years? I got it in the Philippines."

Claire nodded and sipped her coffee. She did not know where to put her gaze. She wanted to take it off his body, but looking at his green eyes was almost worse. They were narrow and intense and shocking in their brightness, brighter than a man's eyes should be. The eyes of a cat.

"So," Owen said. "Not that you need a reason, but why the visit? What's on your mind?"

Claire looked across at him. "I just—I just wanted you to know that whatever you might think about how I feel about you, I'm glad you came back. I know you've probably gotten the impression that I wish you hadn't. But we're family now and I for one am happy that you came home."

Owen did not say anything for a moment and then he began to laugh. A big hearty laugh. He shook his head.

"What?" said Claire.

"No, it's sweet, it really is."

"Listen, I came over here to be nice. To clear up any misunderstanding."

"There's no misunderstanding."

"Good," Claire said.

"Terrific," said Owen, his tone cocky and condescending, and Claire thought, Maybe I spoke too soon. He was being an asshole.

"I didn't come here to get laughed at," she said.

"I'm not laughing at you, Claire."

"Well, it sure feels that way."

"No," Owen said. "I'm not. Listen, I appreciate you coming out here, I do. It's the family thing. That's all. It's not about you. The idea that I have a family still strikes me as, well, not possible. Charlie's my brother and I love him. And I love my mother. But a family is a whole other thing. Something that we stopped being a long time ago."

Claire thought about this. "I'm not sure any family is anything more than a collection of people who happen to be related to one another. Whether it's through marriage or blood."

"Anyway," Owen said, as if that was all, that nothing else needed to be said.

Claire stood. "Thanks for the coffee," she said.

"Stay," Owen said, and his voice was softer now, soft enough that she almost sat back down.

"I should go," she said, and she put on her coat.

"I'm serious," he said. "Stay. I'll be nice. I promise. Plus, I don't get many visitors."

"That's not what I hear," Claire said.

"Ouch," said Owen.

"I'm sorry, I didn't mean anything by that."

"Please stay. Sit."

Claire did as he said. She removed her coat and sat back down.

"You need more light in here," she said.

"I guess I'm used to it. Not many windows on a ship."

"I don't think I could handle that."

"You can get used to anything, I think. With enough time."

"You like living by yourself?"

"I do. I wouldn't be much good at living with someone else. I like my freedom too much."

"So you'll never get married?"

Owen smiled. "Oh, no," he said. "That I won't."

"Never say never, right?"

He leaned his elbows on the table and moved across toward her, tipped his head. "I can say never on that one. Some things you just know."

Claire laughed. "And what about all the hearts you're breaking in Eden?"

"What hearts?"

"All these waitresses and local girls I hear about."

"Ah, those," said Owen, rubbing his chin as if considering this. "You shouldn't listen to town gossip, you know. I'm celibate up here. I'm like a monk."

"Right," said Claire.

Owen leaned back and took a cigarette out of a pack Claire hadn't noticed sitting on the table. He lighted it and inhaled. The smoke filled the air above her and normally she hated cigarette smoke but for some reason now it did not bother her. "It's true," he said, taking his empty hand and laying it over his heart. "I swear."

"Okay, I believe you."

"What about you? You got something on the side?"

"Excuse me?"

"The grocery boy or something."

"Oh, please," Claire said and feigned astonishment but in truth she found herself oddly flattered by this. As if she was the kind of woman who would have affairs. "I'm happily married, thank you."

Owen shrugged. "Married, I knew, happy, I wouldn't have guessed."

"I like being married."

Owen looked at her intently. "Do you though?"

"What do you mean?"

"Well," said Owen, pausing for a moment and looking away, taking a drag off his cigarette. "I'll admit I was surprised as hell to find you here when I got back. I expected Charlie to get married, but to you? No, I didn't see that one coming. Small town, I know. Anything can happen. But what happened to that girl with the big plans? The one who was going to see the world, live in other countries. The smartest girl in school, Claire Apple. Most likely to succeed."

"I traveled," Claire said defensively. "I lived in France. But things are pretty good here."

"You're bored," said Owen. "I can tell."

Claire was stunned. She glared at him and wanted to say "Where do you get off?" but she knew inside that he spoke the truth, that what she thought she kept hidden, in the place she allowed nobody to see, was as accessible to his view as her hair or her eyes.

She said, "Everyone gets a little bored."

Owen smiled. He stubbed his cigarette out in the ashtray and leaned forward. His voice was almost a whisper as he said to her, "What is it you want? What is missing?"

"I don't know."

"You don't know, or you don't want to say you know."

Claire looked at his hands on the table in front of her. She looked at his face.

"I don't want anything," said Claire.

"You mean, you won't say," Owen said.

Claire looked away and was silent.

"It's okay," said Owen. "You don't have to say anything to me."

Claire took a deep breath. She stared at Owen. "You never called."

"I wanted to. I did. Things were just crazy. I needed time and then—"

"It was too late."

"Something like that. The further I got away the harder it was to come back. Doesn't mean I didn't think about—"

"Stop it. Okay. It was a long time ago."

They sat in silence then and Claire wondered if she had said too much.

"I should go now," said Claire, and she stood and put on her coat.

Owen rose as well and for a moment Claire looked up at his face, and she saw something different, a vulnerability, perhaps. But before she could put a finger on it, it was gone.

"Let's do this again," Owen said, and he smiled.

Claire smiled back. She nodded. "Okay," she said.

"I'd walk you out but I don't have a shirt on."

"I think I can make it," said Claire.

"Bye, then," Owen said.

Claire opened the door and walked out into the bright sunshine. She heard the door close behind her and she stood for a moment and looked through the gap in the trees to the leafless hills in the distance. Bright, bright winter sunshine. She climbed into her car. She did not look back. She did not want to see Owen in the window watching her go.

31

On his small patch of earth on the side of Hunger Mountain, Owen Bender sat in a lawn chair and watched winter slowly become spring. He watched the first of the snow begin to melt under the heat of a sun that grew noticeably stronger with each passing day.

In his chair those afternoons before he had to be at the bar, Owen sat and drank cold beer and smoked cigarettes and he saw the geese return in the sky above. He listened to the snowmelt move through the forest. And he thought about things. Again and again he returned in his mind to the Charlotte's of his youth. To the image of his father in front of the large wooden table dicing vegetables, boning fish. His father whom he wanted nothing more than to please, his father whose approval he craved. The image of his mother in the front, his mother with the sun-kissed hair and the eyes he'd inherited from her. And he saw himself and Charlie, inseparable, working, always working, helping out, brothers and best friends, united by both blood and obligation. Of course he had known that nothing lasted forever, that this life of theirs, this family, would inevitably change, as they all do. Still, when he thought back on it what he never imagined was their father leaving them the way he had, and he did not see what would happen after, when it was as if the center could no longer hold and he was sent spinning out into the world to find his place.

Only he never did. He went to the farthest corners of the earth on giant ships, and he saw that on the most fundamental level it was all the same. People struggling with the minutiae of every-day living, of eating and drinking and shitting and sleeping. No matter where he went, he discovered that he was always alone. Even when he was with others, even when he found some strange woman to take to his bed. Especially then. During those years, Owen never felt love, or connection, or anything deeper than the mutual pleasure the sex provided.

Sometimes he blamed Charlotte's for this. For all of them, Charlotte's was their moorings. This was where he figured he and Charlie diverged, for Charlie was still tethered to it, to the place and the food and a woman who felt the same way about it. The structure and meaning it gave to each day. It was Owen and his mother who had had to leave.

Owen did not blame Charlie for any of this. It was true that sometimes he grew angry, especially on days he did not work, when he sat in the trailer or out on the chair and drank the time away until a bitterness came over him that he could not shake. But no, he did not blame Charlie. Charlie was doing precisely what he was supposed to do, what had been handed to him as the chosen one. Owen blamed his father, his father whom he had tried so hard to emulate, only to have him in death take away the one thing that made sense in life. He did not expect to get any of it back. And he did not expect to exact revenge of any kind. Life was not that tidy. But he wanted something. And that spring, he listened to water flow like rain and he tried to understand what would make him whole, what he wanted, what he needed.

OWEN'S DAYS had a rhythm to them, waking late, coffee and breakfast, a light lunch, beer and cigarettes in front of the trailer, work. Some nights he slept alone, other nights he did not, and most Sundays he made his way over to Charlie's for dinner.

He had grown to like these dinners more than he cared to admit. Perhaps it was because it was the season of optimism, the bright northern sun staying in the sky for what seemed like forever, finally setting behind the mountains. And there was the food, always exceptional, and lots of drink and long nights after the boy was in bed of sitting on the old porch and looking at the stars and the moon and talking. Telling stories and talking. Trading stories with his brother and, more important, with Claire, who was the reason that he spent all week looking forward to Sunday.

She was different from other women he had known. She was beautiful, though that alone did not make her exceptional. Owen had known lots of beautiful women. She was different. It was something intangible about her.

Of course, Owen never lost sight of the fact that Claire had married his brother. He could not. On those nights when they had dinner he saw them communicate with each other with the shorthand of husbands and wives; he saw their gentle touch to each other; he saw all of it and it served to remind him that he must give her distance regardless of what he felt, that she was off-limits to him no matter how he felt about her, no matter what they had once shared.

One evening Owen was at work in the kitchen at the bar, pressing burgers together for a rush that would not come, when Sue, one of the waitresses, stuck her head into the small place that he called his own six nights a week. She was a small dark-haired girl with bangs, no more than twenty-two, and she was one of the few who had not made it back to Hunger Mountain with him.

Sue said, "Owen?"

"Yeah."

"Phone."

"Who is it?" Owen said. No one had ever called him at work.

"Some lady," she said.

Owen wiped his hands on a towel and sighed. He went through the swinging doors and into the low-ceilinged bar area. A few regulars at the bar, men drinking Budweiser, some younger kids he did not recognize shooting pool. The Red Sox on the television. A Monday in late June and it was slow.

Owen went to the bar and Karen, an older woman who bartended early in the week, handed him the phone. Owen nodded at her and took it, put it to his ear.

"Yeah?" he said.

"Owen?"

"Claire," he said softly, recognizing her voice. He knew instantly that something was wrong, it was in the muffled way she said his name, as if she had been crying.

"I need your help," she said. "It's Charlie."

His heart leaped in his chest. "Charlie? What, Claire? What about Charlie?"

"He's okay, he is. He's going to be okay. He burned himself."

"What kind of burn?"

"Oil. I don't know all the details. It's all over his left arm. Althea called me. Knocked over a pan full of oil he had used for deep-frying. It's pretty bad, Owen. They airlifted him down to Dartmouth."

"Airlifted?"

"It's the closest burn unit. He's going to be fine. That's what they told me. But I need your help, Owen. I need to go down there. And someone needs to be here for Jonah. He's asleep and I'd ask Althea to do it but she drove to Dartmouth already. I just need someone to be here in case he wakes up. Can you come?"

"Of course, of course. Shit, Claire, I'm sorry. Give me five minutes."

Owen hung up the phone and told Karen at the bar the details quickly and that he was closing the kitchen. Once in his truck, he drove fast down the dirt roads, the night warm and clear, the windows down, and he smoked as he went and he thought about his brother lying in a hospital bed. Owen knew the kitchen could be a dangerous place, just as boats were, and while both he and his brother and their father before them had always displayed nicks from knives on their hands and small burns from picking something up without paying enough attention, bar burns from cookie sheets on their forearms, none of them had ever been seriously hurt. Until now. All that had passed between them now was suddenly irrelevant, and all Owen knew was that his brother needed him, his brother's wife needed him, and Owen could not remember the last time he had been needed by anyone.

32

Owen pulled in front of the house. He got out, dropping his cigarette to the ground, crushing it with the heel of his boot. By the time he reached the porch, Claire was there, and she seemed so relieved to see him, he thought for a moment about hugging her, which was something he had never done, and as soon as he thought it, she did it, wrapped her arms around him, and he held her for a brief moment and then they separated. Owen looked at his sister-in-law.

"Is he okay?" said Owen.

"Yes," Claire said. "He's hurt. They are going to do surgery. Skin grafts. It's a real bad burn. His whole arm. But it's not life-threatening and that's what counts."

"What do I need to know?"

"I put the number of the hospital on the fridge. Althea said she could come back. Jonah is asleep and he will sleep through the night."

"Does he know anything about this?"

"Not yet. I didn't want to wake him."

"All right."

"I'll call. Just stay. Make yourself comfortable. And I can get Althea to come and take your place later if you—"

"No," said Owen. "I'll be fine. I can stay. Just go. Let me know how he is, okay?"

"Thank you," said Claire, and she hugged him again, quickly, and then she was gone. Owen heard her car starting and he stood there until he saw her headlights moving out through the trees and down the drive, fading into the hills.

AFTER SHE was gone, Owen walked through the doors and into the kitchen. It was dead quiet. There was the hum of the clock on the wall and other than that silence. He had not been in the house when it had been like this since he was a child, and even then it was rare that he was alone. Upstairs, Jonah slept without the knowledge of what had happened to his father and Owen wondered what he would tell him if he were to wake. Owen was not someone who related easily to children. They were a mystery to him. He tended to overlook them, the way he did when people had pets. It was not that he did not like children. If he were to think about it, he supposed he would think they were fine, cute and all that, but not his trouble, not his problem. Suddenly, his nephew was both. He needed a drink.

In the buffet in the dining room he found a half-empty bottle of Scotch and poured himself a generous tumblerful. He took a long pull of it and then began to walk. He moved through the living room and to the stairs. He stopped at the base of them and drank again from his Scotch and then he began to walk up the stairs, slowly, not wanting to wake the boy with the creak of the boards under his feet.

At the top of the stairs it was dark and it suddenly occurred to Owen that he had not been upstairs in this house since he was seventeen years old. He had spent his first time back in Eden here but he always slept in the small downstairs bedroom. Beyond that, there was never any reason for him to be anywhere but the kitchen or the dining room or the living room or the porch. He knew that Charlie and Claire slept in his parents' room, straight ahead of him, which meant that Jonah must be in the room Charlie and Owen had shared as boys. He moved toward it, quietly, one foot in front of the other.

When he reached the door, he put his hand on the knob and listened. Silence. He turned the handle and slowly opened the door, remembering that it creaked, and it did, slightly, but then it opened and he stood looking into the room he had slept in as a child. The moonlight streamed through the window that looked out over the pasture to the woods and on a single bed against the wall he could make out his nephew, curled into a fetal position, sleeping. Owen stood and watched the rise and fall of his soft snores. His eyes adjusted to the light but he could not make out Jonah's features. At one point Jonah coughed slightly and he rolled over and Owen thought he was awake, but he saw his arm go up behind his head, surrounding the pillow, and then he heard him snoring again. He stepped back and slowly closed the door.

Out on the porch, Owen finished one Scotch and had another. He smoked and watched the moon. It was at three-quarters and huge in a deep blue sky. A light breeze rustled through the trees and the air was warm.

Owen stayed out there until his next Scotch was gone and then he headed inside. He looked at his watch. It was midnight. No sooner had he come in the door then the phone rang and he looked around for it, realized the sound was coming from the kitchen, and he managed to catch it right before the answering machine picked up.

It was Claire. "How is he?" Owen asked.

"Asleep."

"How bad is it?"

"It's pretty bad but I was able to talk to him briefly. They're going to operate in the morning. Is everything okay with Jonah?"

"He's sleeping, too."

"Are you okay there if I stay the night?"

"Sure. What should I tell the boy?"

Claire paused. "Just tell him what happened. That I will call. But that his father will be fine. That we'll be home soon."

After he hung up, Owen looked down at his now-empty glass and he thought, I should go to sleep. But he decided to have one more drink, one more smoke, and he retired to the porch. He sat down again on the bench and again he watched the moon and the woods and the paleness of the night sky. He was drunk and he was tired but he did not want to go inside. In time his eyes grew heavy and the night gathered around him. He knew he should go in but for some reason he could not. His eyes closed. He slumped against the wall of the old farmhouse, the moon starting its slow descent behind the distant hills.

3 3

Jonah woke him. A light touch on his bare arm and he jerked awake, aware suddenly of bright sun and warm air and the presence of a child to his right. Owen turned and saw him, a little boy with sleep-mussed hair and his mother's dewy black eyes. Long lashes. A handsome kid. He wore pajama bottoms and a T-shirt and his feet were bare.

"Jonah," he said.

"Where are my parents?"

"Jonah," Owen said again, sitting up straight, rubbing his eyes, trying to find the right words. "They'll be home soon. Your father had a small accident at the restaurant but he's fine. They took him to the hospital but there is nothing wrong. Your mother is with him. She'll be home soon. She asked me to cook you breakfast, would you like that?"

"Is he hurt?"

"He's fine. Really. Nothing to worry about. Trust me, he's fine. Your mother should be home by lunch. In the meantime, how about some breakfast? I bet you're hungry."

The boy followed Owen into the kitchen. He was a dutiful and quiet boy and he did not say anything else. He sat at the table, the chair too high for him, his feet dangling, and he looked at Owen expectantly, and Owen was aware of his looking and it unnerved him a little, for he was unused to anyone looking at him that way.

He put the water on for coffee, first things first, then he opened the fridge and looked inside. He saw a carton of eggs and he turned to Jonah and said, "How about eggs?"

The boy nodded.

"How do you like them?"

"Scrambled."

Owen cooked the eggs as his father had taught him to, not as he had done while in the Merchant Marines. He cooked them slow and long, running a spatula through the eggs in the pan, gently stirring them, bringing the curds to the surface. He cooked them until they were light and fluffy and then he and the boy ate wordlessly across from each other, with eggs and toast, Owen drinking coffee, Jonah with a tall glass of orange juice, the silence broken only by the ringing of the phone. Owen looked to Jonah and the boy did not react, so Owen went to it. It was Claire.

She told him the surgery was over, that Charlie was sleeping, and that she was on her way home. Could he stay until she got there? Of course, he assured her, and then he asked Claire when Charlie would return.

"Well, that's the thing," she said. "It'll be at least two weeks. And then he won't be able to work for a while. He wants to talk to you about this. I think I'll let him do that."

"What is it?" Owen said.

"He wants your help, Owen. With Charlotte's. The truth is we can't afford to stay closed that long. You know how that is. The place makes money but doesn't have the turnover or the tables to make a lot. He didn't want me to say anything. But there it is."

Owen shook his head. "I'll have to think about that one," he said.

"Don't say anything to him, okay?" Claire asked.

"I won't," said Owen, and then he brought the phone to Jonah. He could hear Claire's muffled voice and Jonah did not speak as he listened to his mother. Owen watched him as he nodded his head, still chewing on a piece of toast, his feet moving where they dangled.

THE NEXT morning, while a light, warm summer rain fell, Owen drove his pickup the forty miles to the hospital where his brother lay recovering from skin grafts to his left arm. He did not want to visit Charlie in the hospital. He had not been in a hospital since he was born and he shared his father's revulsion for them and for doctors of all kinds. He did not know much about them, other than what he had seen on television and in movies, but he knew they were depressing places, places where people went to die.

But he had promised Claire he would go and talk to his brother, and he knew that he owed Charlie at least this.

At the front desk he asked about Charlie and the nurse asked if he was related.

"I'm his brother," he said.

He took the elevator to the third floor, and when he found the room he was looking for, number 314, he stopped and paused for a moment. Then he opened the door and there lay Charlie, propped up in bed, the television tuned to a talk show. His eyes met Owen's and he smiled. His entire left arm was bandaged and an IV ran into his right arm and he looked tired.

"Come in," he said.

"How are you feeling?" said Owen.

"Like shit. The drugs are strong," he said, motioning to the IV. "They keep them coming."

Owen nodded.

"Sit," said Charlie. "Please. I can use the company."

Owen pulled up a chair. "Where are all the hot nurses?"

"I think that only happens in movies."

"The least they could do is give you a bath."

"No kidding. I think you have to break your legs for that. Oh, man. I fucked up."

"It happens to all of us."

"Not like this," Charlie said. "I'm not even sure how it happened. So fast. I was bending down into the oven and when I came up the whole pot of oil was coming toward me. I jumped back but too late."

"You're lucky it was just your arm," said Owen.

"I know it. Can you imagine if it got on my face?"

"No need to think about that."

"Yeah," said Charlie. "I'm glad you came, I am. Appreciate it. I know it's a long ride. Copley doesn't have a burn unit and these guys are the best around."

"And they give you your own room."

"Yeah, they do that for everybody. Place is like a hotel. Except for the food. The food is awful."

"Can't be worse than Camel's."

"The spaghetti last night was closer to soup."

"Is there anything you need?" Owen said, wanting to get to the heart of the conversation, wanting to say his good-byes and be back in Eden, back at his trailer with his beer and his view of the mountains.

Charlie sighed. "I think I know what you're going to say to this, but I'm going to ask anyway."

"Shoot," said Owen.

"I need your help, Owen. With Charlotte's. It's going to be a month at least before I can cook. Being closed that long will kill us. If it was a week or something, I wouldn't ask. But a month is a long time. You are the only one I can ask. I mean that. The only one who could pull it off."

"What about Claire?"

"She can't do it by herself. She's a great cook but that place gets ripping. The doctor doesn't want me near the place. And I know myself. I couldn't go there without getting in the middle of it. Too much of a control freak."

Owen looked away from his brother, across the bed, to the window. "I don't know, man," he said. "I've been making chicken wings and potpies for twenty years now."

"You're better than that," Charlie said.

"I like what I do."

"I wouldn't ask if I had another choice. You can do this."

Owen ran his hand through his long hair. He looked at his brother, his brother jacked up in a hospital bed, good-hearted Charlie, good-hearted Charlie who knew so little of the world.

"All right," Owen said.

"You'll do it?"

"Yeah. But I don't know any of the dishes, what you're trying to do."

"That's no problem," said Charlie, smiling. "I'll write them out for you."

"Dad hated written recipes, didn't he? He'd probably kill you for that, you know."

"Dad's not here," Charlie said.

34

Later the same day, the soft rain stopped and the sun emerged from dark clouds, and from the doorway of his trailer on Hunger Mountain Owen watched the fullness of the dramatic sky above.

He whittled away the afternoon drinking beer in the lawn chair in front of the trailer and he smoked cigarettes. He had not eaten anything since the eggs with Jonah in the morning and he thought he should eat but he was not hungry. At one point he switched from beer to bourbon and he knew he was getting drunk but he did not care. The day moved on. By sunset, he was in his chair and starting to doze off and the drink was suddenly coming upon him, when he woke quickly because he heard the distinct sound of car tires on the dirt drive leading to his house.

He tried to shake off the drink and the tiredness and then he saw the car, its nose coming between the trees, the Subaru wagon that belonged to Claire. Owen stood and Claire waved from behind the glass as she pulled in front of the trailer. She brought the car to a halt in front of the woodpile and turned off the engine.

When she stepped out of the car, she wore a tight-fitting T-shirt and jeans. Owen became aware of his feet, of his knees, of his thighs, of all that held him erect. He smiled at her. She smiled back.

Claire said, "I brought you something."

"Oh yeah?"

She had a sheaf of paper in her hand and she held it toward him now, moving across the dirt to where he stood. "After you left," she said, "he spent all afternoon writing these down. It was good for him. Gave him something to do."

Claire reached Owen and handed him the loose-leaf unlined paper, all of it scribbled on in his brother's familiar and nearly illegible handwriting. On the first sheet he saw the words *Lobster Charles* underlined.

"The recipes," he said.

"He was so happy, Owen. He'd probably kill me for telling you that. But he was. Knowing that you would help. It means a lot."

"Didn't have much of a choice, did I?"

Claire stood in front of him and she put her hands on her hips and the small wrinkles gathered around her eyes as they did when she questioned things. She said, "Are you drunk?"

Owen laughed. A big, deep-bellied laugh. "Ah, shit," he said. "You got me."

Claire laughed back. "Well, it is summer."

"That it is," said Owen.

"Have you eaten?"

Owen shook his head. "Not since the eggs with Jonah."

"I don't suppose you have any food in this place?"

"I'm sure I could cobble something together."

"Let me," Claire said. "I owe you one."

INSIDE THE trailer, Claire rummaged through his small pantry, looking for something she could put together while Owen sat at his small kitchen table and smoked and sipped bourbon from a tumbler. In truth, she did not know what she was doing here, only that she wanted to be here. Back at the house, Althea had called and offered to come over and help with Jonah, and she was about to say "Don't be silly," but then without thinking about it she found herself accepting and before she could consider it further she found herself driving on the dirt roads on the now-beautiful evening, the air sweet with the earlier rain, and there was nowhere for her to go, for Charlie did not want her at the hospital. He thought it made no sense for her to sit and watch over him when all he wanted to do was sleep anyway, sleep with the benefit of the painkillers. And so she'd ended up here, in her husband's brother's trailer on the flank of a mountain, trying to find something to cook.

She settled on pasta and she put water on the stove to boil. She chopped garlic and opened a can of anchovies and diced these on his cutting board. The only fresh food in the house was a bunch of tomatoes on the windowsill and she diced these as well. In the fridge she found salt-packed capers, the only give-away that he was a chef, everything else, the beer, the carton of eggs, the loaf of commercial rye bread, suggesting someone who lived alone. She rinsed the salt off the capers and chopped these into a rough dice. She sensed Owen watching her but she did not mind. At one point she turned to him and said, "You have anything to drink besides beer and whiskey?"

"Only if you promise to get drunk with me," Owen said.

"No promises," said Claire.

"There's wine under the sink."

Claire opened the small cabinet and next to some bleach and dish soap there were several bottles of red wine and she grabbed one, an Italian Cabernet blend, and she said, "Quite a place to keep your wine."

"Space is at a premium," Owen said. "You have to make do."

Claire opened the bottle, poured herself a glass, and then she began to cook. In a large frying pan she heated olive oil and then sautéed the garlic and the anchovies, breaking up the anchovies with a wooden spoon so that they melted into the oil. Next she added the tomatoes and their juice that had collected on the cutting board and she turned down the heat and softly simmered the tomatoes with the oil and the garlic and the anchovies. The small kitchen filled with the smell of the garlic and while it cooked Claire sipped her wine and when the water came to a boil she dropped a pound of linguini in and salted the water. She added the diced capers to the sauce and finished it with a smattering of red pepper flakes for heat. She drained the pasta and saved some of the water, and tossed the pasta in the pan with the sauce, adding a little of the water to thin it out.

She brought the whole pan to the table and they ate right out of it, with forks and spoons to twirl the pasta on, and outside the night had arrived and Owen lit candles and the intimacy should have been awkward but it was not.

Owen drank wine with dinner and the food seemed to sober him and while they ate they spoke of the restaurant, and it was the first time she had ever talked about the restaurant with Owen, and she liked what he had to say. He told her how men used to come to the restaurant just to get a smile out of Charlotte and how their father knew this but did not mind, for he had never felt threatened by another man his entire life and because he knew it was good for business. He told her stories of the regulars, men like René from Montreal who came in three nights a week, ate at the small bar by himself, and only wanted steak frites, which was not on the menu but which Charles cooked for him anyway, taking a big strip and cooking it *bleu* as requested, barely touching each side to the grill so that the meat was almost as raw as when it was butchered.

"And I think that's why my father cooked him the steak whether it was on the menu or not. He loved that he wanted it *bleu*. Nothing pissed him off more than someone who wanted steak well done. He hated that. Then you get this French guy who wants to eat it raw. There was a purity to that he loved."

"Your father was interesting," Claire said.

"Ah, he was a bastard. But he could cook. Straight-out. Guy could bone a whole chicken in ten minutes. No lie. Ten minutes. He'd turn the thing inside out and you wouldn't even see the knife move. Slice, slice, slice, done. Never seen anything like it."

Claire fingered her wineglass. "I think he would be proud of you. Of both of you."

"But he's not around, is he?" said Owen, lighting a cigarette.

"Part of the reason is what's in your hand," Claire said, and then was sorry she'd said it. "I'm sorry," she said. "I shouldn't have said that."

"No, it's all right," said Owen. "It is the cowardly man's suicide."

And Owen smiled at her then and for a brief moment, as she had once before in this trailer, she saw behind his facade. She saw the boy he had once been, the boy she had known. She saw beneath the surface of the man he was, a man who grew his hair long and kept a scraggly beard so as not to be so pretty. And this was why, when he looked at her with those piercing green eyes and said for the second time, this time with greater force, "Get drunk with me, Claire," she did not go home as she knew she should. She did not stand and leave, walk out the door of the trailer into her waiting car, and drive back the way she had come, back to the old house on Signal Ridge, back to her sleeping child.

Instead, she smiled and said, "I can't," knowing she was not convincing anyone, least of all herself.

At one point, they moved outside and they sat in the lawn chairs under the night sky, clear and full of bright stars. The night was warm and they drank directly from a bottle of wine, passing it between them, and Claire felt it going to her head. It was not often that she drank and she felt now the exuberance and the high that alcohol could bring and she had so much she wanted to say.

Claire told him about being a mother, about how it was amazing, more amazing than anything else she had ever done; how remarkable it was to watch this child grow and see your reflection in his eyes and know that you made him. She talked about the comfort of marriage, about knowing each day that Charlie would be there, that when she rolled over at night it was he who stopped her from rolling off the bed and how there was something to be said for this. And she talked about how all she had ever wanted to do from the moment she set foot in a commercial kitchen was to cook, to create, to work with raw materials and fire and come out with food, great food that made people happy. It was nothing world changing, this work, but making people happy was more than a small thing.

Claire talked because she needed to, and because Owen was there to listen. She was captivating herself with her words, as if she had suddenly discovered that she was full of convictions, opinions, ideas, and all of them needed to rush out her mouth and into the air. It felt good to talk, to be listened to, and even Owen's hand lightly playing with her hair felt all right, it felt like part of the night. Everything was blending into one, and when suddenly she stood, he was in front of her, and before she knew it she was kissing him and his lips were on her neck and his arms were pulling her to him. It was strange and familiar at the same time, his lips on hers.

"Come inside with me," he whispered.

"I can't," said Claire. "I can't."

"Come," he said, and his arms were around her, and his lips brushed across the hairs on the back of her neck and his voice was low and pleading as he said, "Please, Claire, come inside."

Together they stumbled into the trailer. A candle was still lit and this was the only light and it shot long fingers of shadow up the walls and onto the ceiling. They did not close the door. She was against the table and she turned her head away and looked out the door, out toward the blackness that was Eden. She felt him against her and he was hard already and this sobered her, and she said, "No, Owen, I can't, I'm serious."

He looked at her then, and their eyes locked, and he held her by the shoulders. She saw the recognition come into his eyes. He stepped away from her. His arms fell to his sides.

"Jesus," he said, and as he said it his fist came to his face and he hit himself, a blow to the side of his ear. Claire grabbed his arm.

"Don't," she said. "Don't. It's okay, really."

Owen's hands went to his face and he ran them up and through his hair and then down and over his eyes and his cheeks and when they fell again to his sides they were balled as fists and Claire's eyes went to his hands and then up to his eyes, which looked down at the floor.

"I'm sorry," he said, and then he said it again. She moved closer and forced his limp arms around her, wrapped her own arms around his waist.

"It's okay," she whispered.

"I'm drunk," he said.

"I know."

They stayed like this for a while, locked together in the candlelit trailer.

After a time they moved to the bed and Owen lay flat on his back and Claire lay on her stomach and placed her head on his chest.

Soon she heard him snoring and she shifted her weight and turned and looked up at him. She reached her hand up and brushed the wisps of long blond hair away from his face. She began to rise, half kneeling on the bed next to him, and from this position she started to take off his shirt, pulling it up from his stomach, and Owen stirred as she did so and helped her take it off. When it was off, he lay back down and she stood and took off her own shirt and her pants until she was just in her bra and her panties and then she lay back down, her head back on his chest, her mouth next to the small tattoo of the umbrella. They slept.

35

What sleep Owen got was uneven and when he woke it was light in the trailer. He moved slightly and this woke Claire and she slowly turned over and he could see all of her in her underwear and he looked away so as not to be aroused by it.

"What time is it?" she said.

Owen looked at the alarm clock on the nightstand. "A little after eight," he said.

Claire looked up at him, rubbed her eyes. "Ah, my head," she said.

"I know it."

"I need to go."

"Okay," said Owen.

"Do we need to talk?" she asked, her eyes searching, wondering.

"No," he said. "There is nothing to say."

"Yes," said Claire. "There is nothing to say."

She rose then, suddenly trying to be modest, pulling a blanket up with her as she stood, covering her breasts. He watched her wiggle into her jeans, pull her T-shirt over her head, and slip into her sandals. When she was finished she stopped and looked back at him, shook her hair out. Her face was so expressive, sad almost, and he thought that maybe he was wrong, there was more to say than he could put words to, but he could not think of anything and he gave her a weak smile instead.

"Okay," said Claire. "I'm going."

"Claire, wait—"

She stopped. "Yes."

"Thank you."

"You're welcome."

Owen nodded. "I mean it. You helped. You did."

"I know," said Claire.

Owen watched as she opened the screen door and stepped out into the bright daylight. He leaned back and sighed. He lit a cigarette and listened to her car starting up and he felt the haze of the hangover and he knew it would be with him all day.

CLAIRE RETURNED home that morning and Jonah ran to see her when her car pulled in and when he hugged her legs she thought the tears were going to come but she was able to keep them at bay by gritting her teeth. Althea followed the boy and the older

woman mistook the dark circles under Claire's eyes for a difficult night spent in the hospital and she said, "You go take a
bath, get some sleep."

"I can't, Althea, you've been too good."

"Just go on," she said. "Do it."

She knew she did not deserve this self-indulgence but she
was happy to have it, for the hot, soapy water in which she lay,
and from the window she could see Jonah intently working on
something in the yard below, though she could not see what. He
got that from his father, that ability to relentlessly focus, to block
out everything else except the task at hand. Claire wished she
had the same ability, especially now, when later in the day she
would need to visit her husband in the hospital, look him in the
eye, go through the conversational motions that were the heart of
a shared life, all the while pretending she had not spent the
night in his brother's bed. And she would do this, and tomorrow
she would return to Charlotte's, and cook for the first time next
to Owen, and they would act as if they were the same as they
had always been.

OWEN DREAMED of her. She was in his thoughts before he fell
asleep, as he lay with his head on his pillow and stared at the
wall. He knew he would see her in the morning and he knew it
would be awkward but he did not care. He was excited to see
her. Claire. He said her name out loud. He kept imagining her as
she was when he woke in the dead of night and saw her with her
head on his bare chest, the rise of her buttocks beneath the cot-
ton of her panties. He did not want to fall asleep. He wanted con-

trol of his thoughts. He wanted to dwell on her, on seeing her getting dressed, pulling the jeans up over her thighs. He wanted to replay it over and over and he did not want to sleep.

When he woke, he was covered in sweat. He shifted the blankets and flipped his pillow over. He closed his eyes again and tried to remember the dream. There was nothing there.

CLAIRE ARRIVED at Charlotte's a little after nine that morning, getting there earlier than she normally would, leaving the house as soon as the sitter showed up to watch Jonah. She went right to work, taking onions and garlic out of the cooler and beginning the slow process of dicing and slicing them to prepare for the *mise-en-place*. As she worked, she had a sickening feeling in her stomach. She knew it was nerves though it still surprised her: a man had never made her nervous before.

Claire watched the clock above the swinging doors. It seemed not to move. Owen would be here at ten and part of her hoped ten would never come. At the same time, she wanted it to be ten now.

Claire peeled onions and laid them flat and worked through them, filling the white porcelain bowls with neat slices. She watched the clock. She listened for the sound of truck tires on the gravel. She tried to calm the butterflies in her stomach.

As it turned out, however, ten came and went and there was no sign of Owen. Claire was marinating fish and by ten thirty it occurred to her that maybe he was not coming at all, that he had gotten cold feet about working at the restaurant, or that maybe what had happened between them had unnerved him so much that he had left Eden. No, she said to herself, don't be absurd, don't think that. And she shook her head at the thought of it and as she did the door swung open and there he was, his hair pulled back and out of his face, wearing jeans and a long-sleeved T-shirt.

"Hey," he said.

"Hi," said Claire, trying to sound nonchalant, as if nothing was on her mind, as if looking at him did not affect her the way it did.

Owen turned his head and looked at the clock. "I'm sorry, I'm late," he said.

Claire looked away from him, at the onions in front of her. "Don't be silly," she said. "No one punches a clock here."

Owen smiled at her. "You're going to have to show me what to do," he said. "It's been a while."

THEY HAD the work and sometimes the work is all you need. They stood side by side and they prepped and it was as Claire had hoped. There were five entrées and an equal number of appetizers they needed to prepare for, and Claire had forgotten how much she enjoyed this part of the day, and it relaxed her, and in no time the two of them were laughing and joking and she felt the wall between them collapse and they were no different than she and Charlie had once been, years ago, when she first walked through those doors and into the kitchen of Charlotte's.

During the afternoon they had time for a break and they sat outside on the porch so Owen could smoke. The floodplain in front of them was the brightest of greens and beyond they could hear the low rush of the river. Owen smoked and Claire sat next to him and leaned forward with her arms on her knees and at first they did not talk and it felt suddenly intimate, different from the kitchen with the noise of the prep, and Claire was thinking about this when Owen said, "I almost didn't come this morning."

Claire looked at him and then away again. "No?"

"I'll be honest with you, I was scared."

Claire said, "It's not hard. You got right back into it. It's really no different from the other cooking you've done, when you get right down to it."

Owen said, "I'm not talking about the cooking."

Claire fidgeted with her hands. "Oh," she finally said, and she knew what he was going to say and she did not want him to say it for she knew there were times when you should not give words to some things and she wanted this to be one of them. She wished they could pretend that there was nothing between them, that they were not moving toward something that would be difficult to step back from.

"I almost left. Went to Boston. See if I could find a boat. Some fishing work."

Claire reached out now and put one hand on his thigh, felt the muscle tense beneath his jeans. "It's okay," she said.

"I know. I'm glad I didn't go, I am."

"It's going to be okay," Claire said again.

"I think I love you," said Owen.

Claire refused to look at him. She could not. "Don't say that," she said.

"I can't help it," Owen said. "I think I love you."

"Please don't say it," said Claire.

"I have to say it. Some things you can't pretend aren't true. I have to say it."

Claire nodded but she still did not look at him. She focused on one of the slender birch trees on the riverbank. A tall, white pole of a tree, its branches spare near its base, skeletal as it went up, spindly arms shooting off it, its leaves full and green. Claire did not look at him for if she did she thought what he said would become real and that she might cry from the truth of it all. Finally she said, "I'm glad you didn't leave."

And when she said it, she heard him laugh and she turned to see his wide smile, boyish dimples around his mouth. "What?" said Claire.

"That's a start," Owen said. "I'll take it."

Claire couldn't help but smile. "Let's go," she said. "Only an hour till service."

THE RESTAURANT was busy and this made Claire happy. In the bustle of the kitchen she could work from memory, flipping fish and meat on the grill, shaking pan sauces, all the while hearing his words: *I think I love you.* She heard them over and over in her mind and how he had said them, the inflection on the *you.* And as they moved around each other in the kitchen—not bothering to get fully out of each other's way, Owen brushing against the back of Claire as she stood at the grill—she knew that this was what she had wanted to hear. She knew she wanted him to love her. That she wanted to be loved. And not in the way that Charlie loved her, the goodness, the surety of marriage. No, she wanted what she thought Owen could give her, passionate and crazy and not at all interested in consequences or practical concerns. A love that did not care about the future. A love so indulgent and irresponsible that it could not possibly belong to her, Claire Apple, wife, mother, chef. Reliable Claire.

So it was that she first crossed the divide. That Claire realized what she was about to do and knew she could do it, that she had it in her. That she could step outside her life and into another man's arms, and somehow put aside the fact that this man just happened to be her husband's brother.

36

That night, Claire went to the trailer. They had closed the restaurant and they did not talk about Owen telling her he loved her, or say much of anything, really, other than awkward good-byes under the thin light from the crescent moon as they stood in the dark parking lot. Claire saw on his face that he wanted her to say something, that he had said all he could and now it was her turn. But the words did not come, and as she drove back to the old farmhouse on Signal Ridge she hated herself for her cowardice, for her inability to say what she felt, what she decided she could not walk away from.

Then, when she arrived at the house, it occurred to her there was something she could do. The babysitter, a local girl named

Melissa, had dozed off on the couch and when Claire woke her she asked if she would mind spending the night.

"Are you going to the hospital?" asked Melissa.

"Yes," Claire said.

"Sure, Mrs. Bender, I can do that."

"I might actually need you a lot this week. More overnights."

Melissa nodded, rubbed her eyes. She was a good girl, you could count on her. She was solid with Jonah. "No problem," said Melissa.

Upstairs, Claire opened Jonah's door and she stealthily moved across the hardwood floor to his bed. He stirred slightly when she reached him but he did not wake. He was like his father this way and could sleep through anything. His face was pressed into his pillow and his chest moved slowly up and down with the rhythm of sleep. Claire ran her hand through his soft hair, looked at his closed eyes, the long eyelashes any woman would covet. Then she went back out the way she'd come, gently closing the door behind her.

She showered under red-hot water, washing the smells of the kitchen, of the day, off her. As she did, she leaned into the water, letting it run off her long hair, looking to where the water fell to her feet, and she thought of Owen. She thought of his hands, his long-limbed body, of his eyes when he told her he thought he loved her. She saw the way he said it, how much he meant it, the dimples that spread out from his mouth when he laughed. She thought of how the slender pretty boy had grown up to be such a tall strong man. An image of him behind her in the kitchen, his hands on her waist, taking her down to the wooden table, floated into her mind. Claire turned off the water, dried herself off, put on a sundress with a cardigan sweater over it, and within twenty minutes she was driving back down the dirt roads, as if going to Charlotte's.

The night was warm and she drove with the windows down and her hair was still wet and the breeze as it dried it felt good.

Soon Claire was on the Hunger Mountain Road and she slowed down as the car bumped over the washboards and as she climbed up the steep incline. When she reached the cut in the forest that was Owen's driveway, she turned off the lights on her Subaru and took the left turn slowly, moving into the trees and trying to be as quiet as possible. She wanted to surprise him.

She pulled in front of the trailer and her heart sank as she saw all the lights were out. It had never occurred to her that he would be asleep. His truck was here, so she knew he was home.

Then, getting out of the car, she looked toward the door and she saw the glow of his cigarette and then she heard his voice.

"I had hoped you were coming," he said, and she stopped in her tracks.

"You scared me," she said.

"Who was sneaking up on who?" he said, and her eyes had now adjusted to the darkness and she could see his silhouette where he sat on the steps though his face was shielded in darkness and shadow.

"I wanted to surprise you," said Claire.

"Come here," Owen said.

Claire began to walk across the dirt driveway. A breeze blew through the opening in the trees and it was warm and she felt it on her bare legs. She walked slowly, deliberately, and when she got closer, she could make out his face and his eyes. He stared directly back at her. When she was a foot away, he took one last pull on his cigarette and tossed it out onto the dirt and she saw the smoke spill out of his mouth and then his arms were out and around her waist and he pulled her to him. He did not stand and she stood in front of him and they did not speak. She saw that he wore jeans and was barefoot. His hands went from around her waist to underneath the back of her dress and his hands were warm and Claire closed her eyes. Her body arched toward him as she felt his strong hands moving across her buttocks, up her back, and then back down again. His face pressed into her stomach and she let out a slight moan, and then he was rising to stand next to her, and she thought: I will do whatever he wants.

Owen's hand lifted her chin to his face and his other hand was on the back of her head and then gripping a mass of her hair as he kissed her. She kissed him back and he tasted of tobacco but she surprised herself by liking the nutty taste of it against her tongue.

Claire slung her arms around his neck and they kissed and she felt him pulling her up, and she lifted her legs and wrapped them around him, her sandals falling to the wooden steps below.

Owen turned his body and without taking his lips off hers he walked into the dark trailer, half carrying her, his arms holding her up, and he brought her over to the bed and laid her down.

He pulled off her sweater and lifted her dress over her head and she did not need to get ready for him and he seemed to understand. She heard the sound of his belt buckle unfastening and then she felt him against her and in the dark she looked up to where the ceiling was and his face came into focus above her and she closed her eyes.

There was the feeling of him as he pushed into her and there was the quiet hum of the propane stove and there was the sound of his breathing. Claire tried to peel it all away, to relax enough to enjoy the sex, but she could not. Everything felt disconnected and part of her knew that this was the way it was when you made love with someone under these circumstances but the other part of her blamed herself.

"Are you okay?" Owen said from above her.

"It's nice," she said.

"You sure?"

"I just get shy sometimes."

"I don't remember you being shy," he said.

"That was then," said Claire. "Don't tease me."

"You want me to stop?"

"No," she said, "please don't."

He smiled down at her. She smiled back and closed her eyes again, raising her hips to meet him. His hands were on either side of her waist, and this is what she thought of now, his hands, pulling her closer, pushing her away.

OWEN WATCHED her sleep. He wanted a cigarette but he did not want to wake her. Her face was pressed into the pillow, the cheek he could see rosy, her hair falling behind her, her lips slightly agape with quiet breath. Her long nude torso, the side of one breast visible where she met the bed. He was crazy for her. When she first came to him and he sat on the steps with his face buried in her belly, it took all his effort not to sink his teeth into her. He wanted to be patient. He wanted to taste her, wanted to feel the salt of her skin against his tongue.

Now, lying with her naked in his bed while the night passed, Owen was too excited to sleep. He did not want to shut down. He did not want her to leave. He never wanted to see her go out that door again and he knew that was not possible but he thought it anyway.

Sometime later, as the sky turned from blue to dull gray and Eden slowly lightened, Owen decided he could not wait any longer and he woke her. He slid down next to Claire and he kissed the back of her neck and when she rolled over he climbed on top of her and she smiled and ran her hands across his chest and moments later he slid inside her. They made love slowly this time, and they finished with her on top of him and her hair moved in front of his face and outside he could hear everything waking and none of it mattered to him.

37

There is a space that new lovers sometimes find, a kind of cocoon, a place where no one but each other is allowed to enter. And when they are there together, nothing else matters beyond the immediate, beyond each other. There can be no guilt or remorse or concern of any kind. There is only each of you and day bleeds into night and night into day and you go on like this until something shocks you out of it.

They made love so much and slept so little she was constantly sore and should have been exhausted except that nothing could tire her out. One time, when Owen slowed inside her, she pushed him with all her might, and when he smiled lazily at her, she struck him, slapping him hard in the chest with her open palms. He laughed at her.

"What?" Owen said.

"Faster," she said.

There were times, too, of remarkable gentleness. Times when they lay together in the hot postcoital quiet and she would sling one leg over his thigh and they would hold their faces inches away from each other and whisper words of love.

Now and again they laughed and tickled each other like teenage lovers or they wrestled and Owen inevitably got the better of her, and his strong arms and the manner in which he took her down almost always turned her on, and they were back where they started, one, alone together.

One night they stayed late at Charlotte's and they drank wine and while a soft summer rain fell from the night sky they made love sitting on the bench on the back porch. After, they sat side by side with a blanket wrapped around their nude bodies and they looked out toward the woods, toward the river. There was the good wine and the delicious fatigue of the day's work and the lovemaking. All of it lovely and warm and there was nothing else on the entire earth that they wanted, nothing they were missing.

At one point, Owen leaned into Claire and he said, "I don't want this to ever end."

Claire shook out her hair, pushed her thigh into his. "Me neither," she said softly.

"It doesn't have to, you know."

Claire looked over at him. "Let's not talk about it, okay?"

"We have to talk about it sometime."

"But not tonight," Claire said.

"Not tonight, then," said Owen.

She smiled and kissed him on the cheek, and then she rose

from where she sat, dropped the blanket on him, and she stood
naked and laughed and he said, "What?"

"Watch me," she said, and there she went, off the porch and
onto the soft, wet grass of the floodplain, spinning and dancing in
the dark and in the rain, her pale skin luminous in the thin light.
Her hair was matted to her head and her large breasts moved up
and away from her as she spun.

"You're crazy," he said.

"Come get me," she shouted back at him, and she twirled
with her hands over her head, mimicking ballet, the rain falling
steadily, and Owen shook his head at her and stood up himself,
dropping the blanket to the porch, and he stepped out into the
warm summer rain himself, and it felt good on his naked skin,
not at all cold, and he ran to Claire, skipping like a child as he
did, and she saw him coming and shrieked and tried to escape,
but he caught her, wrapped his arms around her. The two of them
naked on the floodplain together and they did not care.

LATE THAT night, neither of them wanted to sleep and they lay in
his bed and listened to the steady thrumming of the rain on the
metal roof of the trailer and Owen told her about the ocean. He
told her about the beautiful sunsets he had seen over the Pacific.

He told her about the magnificent storms, how they humbled
you, how there were nights when he sat in his tiny bunk and listened to the creak of the big boat, felt it listing back and forth
and heard the wind and the water whipping against its flanks and
thought about what it would be like to die out here, to die sur-

rounded by black water and among men he could never say he truly knew. He told her about the days of endless, beating, brutal sunshine. About the oppressive heat of the tiny galley kitchen.

"But you loved it," Claire said.

"Loved it?"

"The ocean."

"No," said Owen. "I don't love the ocean. I respect it. And I loved the ports. Harbors. Working harbors. I love those. And you need an ocean to get to them."

"What a life."

"It was something," said Owen. "Really was."

"Will you go back? Do you miss it?"

"I don't miss the work. But I miss the water. I miss being next to it, seeing it first thing in the morning and last thing before I go to bed. I miss that."

"That sounds nice. A little house on the ocean. Somewhere warm."

"There are places like that, Claire."

"I know it," she said.

"We could go. You could come with me. We could have that."

Claire rolled her head away from him and looked at the wall. He had broken the spell, talked about something beyond the place they had fallen into together. She felt suddenly fragile, like she was made of glass, and when she rolled back toward him her eyes were full of tears.

"I want to," she said.

"We can. Really. We can."

The tears escaped her eyes and she did not wipe at them. She looked at Owen. "I want to," she said again. "But who are we kidding? Who are we fucking kidding?"

Owen reached out and touched her face, with the flat of his thumb stopped one of her tears. He took her head in his large hand, massaged the back of it with his fingers. "I don't want anything but you," he said. "I don't care about anything but you."

Claire looked at him and the tears flowed freely now. "Just hold me, okay?" she said.

He moved closer to her, took her in his arms while he lay and listened to the rain and thought of a small bungalow next to the water, on the Gulf, a place of their own, a fresh start, no history, just the two of them, new and loose onto the world. It would be the life he had always wanted but had not known how to find, and while he knew much stood in his way, it was finally tangible to him now, out there somewhere, waiting for him to grab it.

38

Claire was aware of herself all the time now. Aware of her body beneath her clothes. Her breasts were sensitive as they had been after giving birth and she could barely move without thinking about him and the slightest of things aroused her and she worried that it showed. That everyone she saw in town or at the restaurant knew the kind of woman she was, the kind of woman who could run around with her husband's brother, the kind of woman who spent her nights in a trailer on the side of a mountain.

Part of her enjoyed this feeling. She saw the way other men looked at her and she knew they desired her and it had been a long time since she had noticed men looking at her. Sometimes she thought they probably always had but other times she realized that it was what she gave off to them now. That she wanted to be desired. What woman did not? And Owen desired her, no question. He could not get enough of her. But he also loved her and Claire knew this was where it got difficult, for she loved him, too, and she was smart enough to know that loving him was a luxury she did not have.

At the same time she thought: Love is not something one can control. You cannot turn it off like a faucet. You cannot pretend it is not there. Like little else in life, it is an absolute. There is no room for ambiguity.

And when she thought this, she grew sad. Claire knew that in time all of it would need to be addressed and such things seldom came to a good end. And for this reason, she tried to put it out of her mind and, in general, she succeeded. When she was at Charlotte's there was the work and there was Owen. At night, it was just her and Owen and in his embrace she went to the place she wanted to be, where her mind emptied and all that mattered was what they did in their particular sliver of time: they had no future, no past, only the limitless present.

Sometimes, though, she'd return home in the morning to see her son, the boy she and Charlie had made, Jonah, sitting at the table eating his breakfast, and she'd see in him his father and it was like a blow to her gut. He was so young and perfect and tied them together as nothing else could, as nothing that she had with Owen would. And then, of course, there were the conversations she had with Charlie, where they talked about the restaurant, about his healing, and often about Owen, and she had never betrayed him before and it bothered her, though she knew that regardless of what happened, he could never know about her, he could never know about Owen, about the two of them.

While he was in the hospital, she talked to Charlie twice a day. She set the schedule and she counted on it, for this way he could not find out where she was spending her nights. She called him both times from Charlotte's, in the morning when she arrived before Owen, and again at night after service and while Owen was out on the porch smoking. She amazed herself with how easy it all seemed, that this was her life; how good she was at the deception. And then one morning Charlie told her what she was blocking out, what she was afraid to hear.

He told her they said he could go home.

"When?" asked Claire, trying to sound enthusiastic.

"Two days. I can't wait, Claire. It'll be so good to be home."

"Ah, Charlie," she said. "That's great. We've missed you so much."

"Of course it'll be a while before I can work again. But one thing at a time. It'll just be nice to be back in Eden. Back with you. And to see Jonah."

After she hung up the phone, Claire slumped into one of the chairs in the dining room. She ran her hand through her hair and suddenly she could hear her heart beating in her ears, in her throat as well, until it seemed all she could be was heart, throbbing, beating heart. She tried to catch her breath but it was hard. It came in ragged gasps and she was scared, really scared, more scared than she had ever been. She gripped her face in her hands and she wanted to be somewhere else, far from here.

Claire sat in the chair and looked around the small dining room, with its tangerine walls and its square tables, and in time she heard the sound of Owen's truck tires on the driveway. She rose and went to the kitchen, to the work, determined to pretend for now that nothing had changed. She would try to buy herself some time, see if she could figure things out.

ALL THAT day she kept the news of Charlie's return to herself. The news of it swirled around in her mind, though if it showed outwardly, Owen did not say anything to her as they worked together. It was a slow night and they were able to close a little early, and Claire drove home to the house on Signal Ridge and checked on the babysitter, and on her sleeping son, and then she took a shower. An hour later she was back at Owen's trailer and while they sat outside on the lawn chairs she told him about Charlie's release.

As soon as she finished speaking, Owen sprang out of his chair and stood over her. A cigarette dangled from his mouth and he took his beer bottle and in a moment of pure rage hurled it with his right hand across the driveway where Claire heard it shatter against the woodpile.

"Fuck," he said.

Claire looked straight ahead and she did not say anything. She sat still and she could feel his rage all around her, electric and coming off him in waves. She finally said, "How do you think I feel?"

"I know," he said.

"This should hardly be a surprise, Owen. I mean, what did you think, that they were going to keep him there for a year?"

"I know. I know. I just. I guess I'm not ready for it, that's all."

Claire sighed. "It's terrible," she said.

"It doesn't have to be," said Owen.

"How?" said Claire, and she said it like she meant it, like he had the power to change things.

Owen got down in front of her in the dark. He stubbed out his cigarette on the ground and he knelt facing her, supporting himself with his hands on the arms of her chair. He stared at her in the dim light.

"We could go," he said. "Me and you. We could go. Leave here. Start something together. Build a life—

"We could. We really could. I mean, I'm not fucking around with this, you know? I love you, Claire, I do. And that means more than anything. With that, nothing can stop us, don't you see? We just have to think differently. That's all."

Claire shook her head and looked away from him. She looked toward the woods across the road to her left, a different shade of blackness in the night. "It's so easy, isn't it?" she said, her voice betraying her sarcasm.

"It could be," Owen said brightly. "Listen: do you love me? Answer me that."

Claire turned back to him, her sarcasm gone now, and she looked at him, at his handsome face. She did not hesitate and her words surprised even her with how easily they came to her. She said to him, "Yes. Yes, I do."

"Then what can stop us? It seems to me that this is the only thing we can do. And I tell you one thing: I won't sit here and watch you pretend to be with my brother when you should be with me."

"Jesus," Claire said. "What does that mean?"

Owen stood up. "I don't know," he said, and Claire could sense his anger again and she had never seen him like this and it frightened her. But then he realized she was scared and he knew enough to step back. She felt him calming down before he spoke.

"It doesn't mean anything," he finally said. "I just don't know what to do, Claire. I've never felt like this before, you have to understand that. I need you."

His voice was softer now and Claire said, "This is hard for me. I have a son. A husband. Jonah. Charlie. I don't know what to do. How can I leave them?"

"You know I can't help you with that. All I can say is that I love you."

Claire shook her head again. "I don't know what to do," she repeated.

"Think about it, okay? Just think about it."

Claire reached out and tousled his hair. "Okay," she said, and she meant it.

They barely slept that night. Neither of them wanting to give in to sleep. They made love with a fury they had not felt before.

Eventually they lay side by side and Owen wrapped his arms around Claire and she leaned into him and they did not speak. The premorning was cool and Owen pulled a blanket over them and in the cold of the breeze that came through the window Claire sensed the first taste of autumn and the winter to follow and she thought then of a small house on the ocean, of the life that Owen had said could be theirs. She thought about what it would be like to spend every day with him. She thought about sunsets over the endless ocean and the two of them growing old together but never losing the passion that fueled them. She thought about the anonymity that would come from a new place. The control she would have over a new life.

And as Claire thought this, as she lay in the crook of his arm and watched the gray of morning begin to come through the narrow windows, she decided that maybe it was possible after all, that you could risk it all for love, that maybe, if given the opportunity, you had to risk it all for love. That sometimes you had to give up a tremendous amount to find what was truly important. Nothing good comes cheap, as her father used to say, though admittedly when he said such things it was never the heart he was talking about. In this case, the price for love was enormous, maybe unthinkable, but in the end, did she really have a choice?

Owen shifted his weight and Claire rolled to face the wall. He wrapped his arms around her and she felt his knees underneath her own. His left hand slid down and rested on her bare belly, his palm opening up. It was warm. She tried to imagine that hand pulling away from her soft skin and never coming back.

39

They were subdued that next day in the restaurant kitchen as they worked. Part of it was the exhaustion, the hour or two of sleep they were able to find after a night they did not want to end. Part of it was the weight of thought that they both now collectively carried, what they had settled on in the first gray of morning. What they had agreed upon when they knew they had to agree upon something.

Owen was surprised when Claire told him she would go with him. In the week or so he had been thinking about it, it had always been more fantasy than something that seemed possible. Oh, he wanted it to be true. He wanted to believe that the two of them could leave together, could walk out of Eden and only look forward. But he also knew they each had their history here. And for Claire, a family that was hers, a child no less, and a life outside of him that could not be denied no matter how badly he wanted that to happen.

And then there was Charlie, his brother, the man who let Owen back into his life when he probably had not earned that kind of trust. Years of escaping into the world only to return and take Claire back like no time had passed. Didn't he owe Charlie more than that?

Yet when Claire told him she would go, he saw all of it and suddenly the absurd appeared plausible. His reservations moved into the back of his mind as he saw their future together. As he saw happiness.

Owen could tell how scared she was, though he could also tell that she was equally scared of losing him, of what they now had, and he found comfort in this, and the more they talked about it, the more their words started to bring this idea, this plan such as it was, into being.

It was Owen who had proposed that they leave right away.

"It's the only way," he told her. "A clean break. You pick up Charlie tomorrow and then we work and after we leave right from Charlotte's. It will be a long time before anyone knows we are gone. Probably the next morning. Maybe the middle of the night if Charlie wakes up. But by that time, we'll be halfway to Florida."

"I don't think that will work," said Claire.

"Why not?"

"He'll stay up for me. It's his first night back. I think he would get suspicious."

Owen scratched his chin. "The next morning, then. Here at Charlotte's. We'll just not open that day."

"It's crazy," Claire said. "It's so crazy."

"We just have to get through the next two days. Then it gets easy. It will be so good. It will. I need you to trust me, though, Claire. Can you do that? Can you trust me?"

"Yes," Claire said, "I can trust you."

"Good," he said. "This can work."

And then, working in the kitchen, Owen watched Claire and he knew the sobriety of daylight was taking its toll on her. It was also taking its toll on him but he refused to acknowledge it. He did not want to dwell on what they were going to do: he simply wanted to do it. He had faith in how he felt for her. It was, he sometimes thought, the only truly genuine thing that had ever happened to him.

That night, their last together before Charlie returned to Eden, they slept the bone-tired sleep of the exhausted and even if they had wanted to make love they could not. They rolled into each other and though it was a cold night they left the windows open in the trailer. Cool air ripped through the slat windows. They rubbed their bodies together under the heavy blankets and they ignored the rain and the cold and what stood in front of them. Everything was about to change as clearly as the summer was about to become fall. No one knew how it would turn out. All they could do was keep warm, keep each other warm, welcome the sleep when it came, and listen to the rain.

40

In the morning the rain had stopped and a dense fog hung in the green valleys of Vermont as Claire drove to Dartmouth to pick up Charlie. There were few cars on the highway at this time and as she drove she looked at the fog-filled valleys, sometimes getting a glimpse of hills and small towns in the distance, the occasional white steeple of a church rising up below the highway. Behind the wheel of the car she felt suddenly alone in the world, steering up and over these long hills, and she was scared to see Charlie. She wondered how obvious it was, her and Owen. She wondered if she smelled like him, like his cigarettes, if she wore his scent on her clothes. She wondered if her betrayal showed in her face, if Charlie would see it in her eyes and know right away what she had done, and what she was about to do.

At the hospital, she met him outside his third-floor room and he was all ready for her, sitting in a wheelchair, talking to one of the nurses. He looked the same as he always had and his arm was bandaged and she felt a shiver run through her when she bent down and kissed him.

"Charlie," she said.

"Can you believe it's my arm and not my leg and I have to be wheeled out of here?" he said with a playful shrug. "It makes no sense."

"Those are the rules," said the nurse.

Claire wheeled her husband out and into the day, which was slowly clearing. As soon as he reached the pavement, he stood and said, "That's better. Damn, it's good to be free."

Charlie put his good arm around her and Claire moved into him for a moment before they separated and headed into the parking lot to the car.

The whole ride back, Charlie wanted to talk. He was full of questions, one after another. Questions about Jonah, about the restaurant, about deliveries and suppliers, about money and menus, and, yes, about Owen. Claire felt like each word she spoke was a betrayal, and especially when she spoke of Owen. He wanted to know how Owen was adapting in the kitchen and Claire told him he was better each passing day, and she surprised herself with the ease of her words, as if she were talking about someone they had hired, not his brother, her lover, the man she was about to leave him for.

The trip took almost an hour, and by the time they reached the house on Signal Ridge, Claire was exhausted. As they pulled into the driveway, Claire saw that Jonah was outside and she looked at Charlie and noticed his face brighten and when he looked this way she suddenly felt a twinge of deep love and regret, and she saw him in that moment as she used to see him, long ago, when they were first together, the Charlie who loved her so easily, the Charlie who had brought her into his kitchen, his life.

Claire parked the car and Jonah ran to his father and Charlie said, "Whoa, easy, buddy, bad arm," and then picked him up anyway with his one good arm, swung the boy around, and Claire fought off tears and looked away toward the woods.

An hour later she was at Charlotte's and she was grateful to be here, away from her guilt. She arrived before Owen and when he walked in the door she went to him, wrapped her arms around him, and he whispered to her, "It'll be okay."

They had much work to do but she needed him that morning and they made love in the pantry, and it was cramped and awkward but she wanted to feel him and she wanted to move and to sweat and to not think.

They worked in silence most of that day and that night the restaurant was busier than usual and they turned out entrée after entrée, working side by side, efficiently, yet talking little. They both knew that tonight they would separate, they would sleep away from each other, and in the morning they would leave Eden behind, Claire for the second time, Owen for the last.

Despite the frantic pace in the kitchen, the night seemed to drag on endlessly. Claire tried to think only about the work but she knew she wore her thoughts on her face and she kept having to remind herself to do things that normally came naturally: smile at the waitresses, banter with Joe Collins, pretend Owen was just another cook, someone she worked with.

When they were finally finished, Claire turned down the

lights and locked the doors before meeting Owen out in driveway where he had gone to smoke. Outside, it was growing cool. Owen stood by his truck and as Claire walked toward him she could see the glow of his cigarette. She folded her arms over her chest against the cold, and when she reached him, they did not speak right away and Owen smoked and she looked past him up the road and listened to the sounds of the night river cutting through the trees.

Finally Owen tossed his cigarette out into the grass and Claire said, "Hug me," and he did, moving into her and taking her into his arms. They stayed like this for what seemed a long time, not moving, a light cool breeze blowing on her hair. Eventually Claire pulled away first, leaned up and kissed him on the lips, tasting his tobacco.

She said, "It's going to be hard tonight. Being away from you."

"I know it," said Owen.

"Tomorrow, then?"

"Tomorrow," he said.

Claire nodded at him. "I love you," she said, shrugging her shoulders for she did not know what else to do.

"I love you, too," said Owen.

Claire nodded again, stuffed her hands into the front pockets of her jeans and got into her car, drove back to her family, to the life she was about to depart.

OWEN HAD the whiskey and he had his cigarettes and the dark in front of him as he sat on the steps of the trailer and wished the night away. Tomorrow was going to come quick and he found it easiest if he tried not to think about it, though he could not help it. The leaving haunted him. He thought about Claire, how she made him feel, how she opened him up, so that he did not feel guarded around her: for the first time in his life he felt like he could be himself, that in front of him lay a future where he would know what it meant to be happy, truly happy, as he sometimes naively imagined most of the people he knew were.

But in the dark, cloud-filled night, he also thought of Charlie, his brother, once his best friend, and it made him angry that he could not think of Charlie without also now thinking of Claire and her relationship to him. Why hadn't Owen married her first? How uncomplicated would that have been? Maybe he could have had both, his brother's friendship and Claire's love. For deep down, was that not what he wanted?

Owen sat and drank and ignored the gathering cold. At one point a great breeze came down across the ridgeline and the trees in front of him bent under its strain. The clouds opened up above and the moon appeared. The summer was short. Fall was coming. Fall was almost here. He drank the amber whiskey and he steadied himself for sleep. He did not want to dream. Not to-night. He did not want to dream.

AT THE old farmhouse, Claire turned off the remaining lights and closed the open windows in the living room and climbed the stairs. She stopped first at Jonah's room, opened the door slowly, and saw that he had fallen asleep with his light on. She went and turned it off and then sat on the bed next to him for a moment. He stirred and she ran her hand through his hair and he smiled slightly, aware of her touch, and she wondered how much he knew about her absence the last few weeks. Claire bent down and kissed him on the cheek, pulled his blankets up a little, and left him in the dark.

In the bedroom she shared with Charlie, the lights were already off and she could hear him snoring softly. She stepped gingerly to her closet and took off the kitchen clothes, put on pajamas. It was strange to wear pajamas again. She had grown so used to wearing nothing to sleep. As quietly as she could, Claire lifted the blankets on her side of the bed and climbed under the covers with Charlie. His snoring changed rhythm for a moment but then he was back at it again. She rolled over away from him and she wished she had some kind of sleeping pill or something since she knew rest would probably elude her this night. She wondered what Owen was doing and if he was thinking of her the way she thought of him. Behind her, Charlie stopped snoring and Claire froze for some reason, as if he were a stranger, as if she had suddenly realized someone else was in the room. And in a moment he moved into her from behind and she knew he was awake and it was suddenly the familiar feel of him, her husband, and in that moment she knew that the love had not left them completely, the quiet love of the married, a love that paled in intensity to what she had with Owen.

"Hey," he whispered to her. "When did you get here?"

"A half hour ago."

"Ah, you were quiet."

Charlie slung his one good arm over her and said, "It's good to feel you."

She said, "I have my period." She felt him go still behind her.

"Bad timing," he said lightly.

"I know," Claire whispered.

She felt his lips on her neck and he said, "I love you."

"Yes," said Claire, and she knew it was not what she was expected to say but she also knew he would not catch it and he did not. In a short time she heard his snores again, the steady rise and fall of his sleep.

Claire listened to the harsh cold wind rattle the old twelve-pane windows. She listened to Charlie snoring and suddenly the last three weeks felt like a dream, some kind of strange dream. Her husband was behind her, her child in the other room, a child they had made, a child she was responsible for, and this house, this house that had once belonged to her husband's parents, was hers now. This was how it had been for a long time. Together it was a life, and it might not be a perfect life, but she had built it and she thought: I cannot do this. All love eventually flamed out, didn't it? Was anything permanent? Wouldn't she someday find herself lying next to Owen and feel the same way she felt about Charlie? Oh yes, she thought, what she had with Charlie might not be exciting, but there was something to be said for the quiet love of two people who had been together forever, the ease they shared, where she did not ever worry about him, where she took him for granted, not as that sounded, but in a positive sense, in the way you come to rely on the snow of winter and the heat of summer, on the solid warmth of a great meal. He would always be here for her, and did he deserve this, what she was about to do?

But then she thought of Owen and she remembered the feel of his hands on her, the way he looked at her.

Lying there that night with Charlie beside her, Claire hoped for sleep. She tried to find an image to hang on to, one that would carry her through, give her the smallest semblance of peace she thought she needed to move forward, to do what she thought her heart ached for her to do. It came in the form of a vision, more than an image, and for a brief moment it allowed her to forget that she had decisions to make. She saw the house she and Owen had spoken of, a small place where a river met the sea, a simple Cape, with a wide porch that looked out onto the bright, sun-splashed ocean. It was just the two of them and the water and the salt spray on days when the wind blew vigorously. All of it was light and beautiful and as possible as Owen had said it could be.

41

Sleep was elusive and would not come the way he wanted it to. There were the memories that were unloosed upon him. He could not run from his past anymore. Some things were immutable and that night he saw all of them. He saw himself and Charlie, and he saw his beautiful, gracious mother, and he saw the specter of his father. He saw the boy he was and the man he had tried to become. He saw Claire, wonderful Claire, soulful-eyed Claire, the one who had allowed him to make the decision he was about to make. Time had passed and they had all changed—the world had changed around them—and he knew that whichever direction he went in when the sun rose would determine what would become of all of them. He had that power. He wanted to choose right.

Owen did not remember going to sleep but when he woke there was bright sunlight. His mouth was dry and he paused for a moment to gauge the hangover. He had drunk almost a fifth of whiskey and he had got his wish: there were no dreams, though now his head throbbed and it took a second to remember what it was this day meant, and as soon as he did he rose out of the bed and tried to pull himself together. He went through the motions of the morning, grinding beans and making coffee, checking the weather out the door while he smoked a cigarette. The coffee helped, as did a long shower that he took with the water as hot as he could stand it. When he had finished he placed a towel soaked in cold water around his forehead and when he dressed he felt more like himself, more like he was up to the challenges that the next hours would bring.

Owen forced down stale toast after his coffee and he packed one duffel bag and left everything else in the trailer. He did not care what happened to it.

By the time Owen climbed into his truck he figured he was running late, but when he looked at the clock he realized it was not even ten. He was early and that was okay, too, for he wanted to wait for Claire, and not the other way around.

He drove under the bright blue sky down the dirt mountain road and out onto the Old County Road. He drove and he smoked and he thought. He was aware of his heart now, as if it were all he was, the steady beating of it, blood flowing through him, his limbs leaden with weight he could not explain.

As he rounded the bend and the road opened up there was Charlotte's on the side of the road, in front of the floodplain, and it occurred to him that this might be the last time he would ever see it. Even when he was in other parts of the world, he had always known he could come back here. Now Owen figured that possibility was no longer his. He pulled into the parking lot. He stopped the truck and stepped out.

Owen stood next to his truck and he looked down the long narrow valley that led to Hunger Mountain. He turned and looked at the small schoolhouse, the red door, the chimney, and behind it the floodplain and the river. It was a beautiful spot and he saw it this morning as others might see it, as his father had seen it many years ago on a hunting trip from New York, a trip when he had decided he had to have it. It made sense here, it all fitted together. The schoolhouse on the river, the valley, the mountain standing watch over all of it. It had been his father's and his mother's and now it was Charlie's. It was never going to be Owen's and he knew that now. And that was okay, he thought, for some things were more important than restaurants, regardless of what his father might have thought. Claire had taught him that, and feeling the sun warming his skin, he was grateful for knowing it.

As he stood waiting for her to arrive, all of him hurt and he knew it was not about to get easier. He had done difficult things in his life, though they had been things he had done for himself and himself only. This was different and he knew that but it did nothing to soften what he was about to do. He braced himself.

Owen turned back toward the road and he heard her before he saw her, the distinct sound of car tires on the hardened dirt road. Her Subaru came around the bend and she pulled into the parking lot and came to a stop. There she was through the glass and she smiled at him and he was too far away to see how clenched her smile was, though he suspected that she was feeling this as much as he was, probably more.

Owen watched as Claire got out of the car, opened the back door, and took out a duffel bag not unlike his own. Her hair was down and she wore a white T-shirt and jeans, the men's work boots she wore when she cooked. The sun caught her face just right, her hair and her eyes, and he felt something give within himself. Owen smiled as she walked toward him and she smiled back and he saw now that she had been crying and before he could say anything she said, "It's all going to be okay, right? Tell me it's all going to be okay."

Owen watched her come to him. When she was a foot away, he said, "It's all going to be okay."

Claire dropped her bag on the ground and she stood in front of him and there were lines on her forehead, crow's-feet and lines that shot out from under her eyes, and in the bright sunlight he saw the first strands of silver in her hair and he had never noticed them before. She was more remarkable than she had ever been and he looked at her and he knew she was about to hug him and he needed to say what he needed to say before she did. He needed to tell her what he had decided and the words when they came were distant to him, as if being uttered by someone else.

Owen said, "You're not coming."

Claire looked puzzled for a moment, her eyes widening, and then Owen saw her face go slack and he expected the anger to come then. He expected her to hit him. Instead, her body suggested resignation and she looked away and he heard her sobs and the slight choking in her throat when one cries too hard and when she spoke it was almost a whisper, her voice low and husky. She said, "I know."

"You brought a bag," said Owen.

"I didn't know until I got here."

Owen nodded. "It was a long night."

"Me too," said Claire, and she looked back at him now and the tears filled her big dark eyes and he wanted her tears to go away.

"You belong here," Owen said. "You do. You know it as much as I do."

"But so do you," she said. "Why are you different?"

"You know I can't stay."

Owen stepped toward her. He placed his hands on the outsides of her arms and she was sobbing hard now and she felt as frail as a bird to him, as if she might collapse under his touch. "It's okay," he said. "I was part of this place once but no longer. And sometimes it's hard to figure things out. I don't belong here, Claire, I don't. I don't know where I'm supposed to go. Maybe the ocean, maybe not. But I know now that it's not here and that I cannot take you with me. Charlie loves you. He deserves you. And as much as it hurts me to know this, I know you love him, too. I've seen it. I saw it the first time I saw you together. The way you looked at him."

Claire looked up at him and she wiped hard at her eyes. "I love you," she said, and her arms fell to her side and as she rocked slightly Owen put his arms around her and pulled her to him, and he saw that she was biting her lip, but still the tears would not stop. He held her as hard as he could, as tightly as he could. She shook in his arms. He was happy to hold her for it allowed him to ignore the fact that he felt like he might crack himself. He could take care of her and pretend that he did not hurt as bad as he did, as bad as he ever had, and by so doing he kept himself from completely falling apart.

"What's going to happen to us?" Claire asked into his chest.

"We're going to be fine," Owen said. "We're all going to be fine."

He held her tighter, his face pressed against the top of her head, his own tears leaving his eyes.

IN THE end, Owen knew it was the only thing to do. The night before he had not had to worry about dreams for the sleep would not come and he sat haunted by his thoughts, by his memories. He stayed up most of the night, and as he imagined and wished for a life with Claire, he saw the lives left behind, he saw Charlie and he saw Jonah and he knew Charlie had done nothing to him that could equal what he was about to do. Yes, Charlie had got the restaurant, but you could not possibly compare a building, a business, with the love of any woman, let alone a woman like Claire. No, thought Owen, he had done nothing to deserve her, to deserve her grace and her beauty, and as much as he wanted her, he knew he could not have her. Her life was here with Charlie, with her son, their family, and maybe Charlotte's had already taken one family apart, maybe this was what that business did, but Owen, looking out into the blackness and drinking his whiskey, was not ready to see it take another. He owed his brother more than that and it had taken him a long time to realize this. He owed Claire more than this as well.

Instead, he decided he would leave again, and like the first time, he would leave alone. Though he also was wise enough to understand that this was where the similarities between his youth and now ended.

The first time he left he was just a boy and he knew nothing of the world and he set out because he hurt and because of the pain and he chose the life he did because he wanted to keep moving, as if in the constant motion he did not need to be open to anything, he could stay closed to all but those things right in front of him: the ocean, the expanse of ship, the galley kitchen, smoking under the great arch of stars at night.

Now he would leave and he would leave with an open heart, a heart opened by Claire and when your heart is open you cannot only think for yourself. You learn to love as well as to see, and when you learn to love, you learn that love carries with it responsibility and an obligation to do your best.

This was what Owen realized that night. Suddenly his choices were clear.

In the parking lot that morning, Owen did not leave Claire until he was certain she would be okay. He held her as long as he could. It took everything he had to hold it together and he knew he could not last for long. When he finally got into his truck and drove out of the parking lot he told himself not to look back, Just don't look back, he thought, but it was not that easy. There was so much behind him and he needed to look. It was only human. And so he did and he saw Claire standing next to her car, and he saw Charlotte's behind her, and he saw the trees and a ribbon of the river and it was all he needed to see. Above him the sun shone brightly and on the hills in front of him he could see the first sign of color, a touch of red here and there. It spoke of things to come, the change that this time of year always brought. He drove fast, pushing the truck around the corner and out of sight, following the Dog River as it ran away from the mountains, as it ran out of Eden.

EPILOGUE

They came with regularity, every six months or so, though they were in envelopes now, and he took the time to tell them about his house, how he had had it built on stilts so that the tide could roll right under it. He told them about the redfish he caught in the brackish water that ran through the tidal river. He wrote about the sunrise, how he never got tired of watching it rise up over the water, its golden light on the flowing reeds at the mouth of the river.

For their part, it was Charlie who responded. Charlie who wrote Owen and told him to get a phone like a normal person so they could talk more regularly, not only when they had time to write letters. It was Charlie who asked him to come back to Eden.

But both of them knew he would probably not take them up on

the offer, though Charlie held out hope. Claire fully expected never to see him again.

The summer after Jonah turned sixteen he began to work at the restaurant. He was a tall, gawky kid, with his mother's eyes and his father's build, though he had not filled out yet. Charlie and Claire told him he did not have to be in the restaurant if he did not want to, but Jonah insisted it was what he wanted to do and at night lying in bed Charlie and Claire would talk about it, and when Charlie suggested it would be better if he worked somewhere else, if he had a chance at a different life before he committed to the one they knew, Claire said, "We shouldn't choose for him. It's what he wants."

And so they taught him, as Charlie had been taught. Every morning that summer, Claire gave her son blind baskets and she saw that he had the gift, the intuitive gift that his father had, and that she had been told his grandfather had as well. He saw the dishes in front of him as soon as she lifted the towel off the basket, and when Claire watched him cook, watched him follow with great logic the movement from raw ingredients to finished food on the plate, she was humbled by it.

In her son she saw herself as she had been many years ago, when she walked through the doors of this old schoolhouse and fell in love first with a restaurant and then second with a man. She remembered how everything had felt back then, how it felt to wake every morning and want to be in this warm room with its view of the river, the light streaming through the windows onto the old wide-board floors. She remembered how it felt to get better each day, to learn from Charlie. She remembered how much she loved the heat of the stove, the agile play of cooking so many dishes at once, her personal high-wire act. And she remembered how tired she was at night, the delicious kind of tired where you know you have worked hard, where you knew you have earned the tired and the day was a day you were proud of. By watching her son, by overseeing his apprenticeship, she realized she could feel all this again, feel it through his eyes.

And in her heart, Claire knew she had Owen to thank for this. He had come to her at a time when she had fallen asleep and he had woken her. There were times when she missed his touch, the grace of his lovemaking, but that was mostly long ago, when he first left and there were nights that she lay in bed and remembered what it was like to be with him. Where she closed her eyes and imagined him moving over her. Nights when she wondered about him, where he was. This was before the letters started, letters that when they came she stole from Charlie and read over and over again in the tub.

In time she came to see his true gift to her. He had allowed her to be at peace, to know what she had. He had taught her to see again. To believe again. He had shown her how to love.

Claire understood that she had helped him, too, that in her arms he had found what he needed to move on, to escape the past. What they had shared belonged to a particular moment. Claire did not want for anything. She had a good husband, a good house, a good restaurant, a good son, a good life. She had made mistakes but in time she forgave herself. Charlie needed her. Jonah needed her. Charlotte's needed her. Eden was her home.

Everything was right here.

ACKNOWLEDGMENTS

I would like to thank the following:

Claire Wachtel, my editor at William Morrow, who taught me more in two weeks about my writing than I learned in two years of graduate school. Kevin Callahan, also at Morrow, who has been a great supporter of this book.

My agent, Nick Ellison, patron and friend, who works twenty-four hours a day to help my work find an audience. Also Sarah Dickman, Kate Flynn, Abby Koons, and Jennifer Cayea at Nicholas Ellison, Inc. I truly appreciate all your efforts.

My wife, and first reader, Tia McCarthy, to whom this book is dedicated. You carry my heart in every way.

My early readers: Maura Greene, Daniel Greene, Susan

McCarthy, Jennifer O'Connor, Karen Kesselring, Margaret Gendron, and Alex Lehmann. Your advice was invaluable.

As always, I want to thank my parents.

I am also indebted to John McPhee's excellent book *Looking for a Ship*, for helping me understand the Merchant Marines.